# Ex Nihilo

## A Unity Chronicles Novel
### by Nick Westwood

The Unity Chronicles can be found on Facebook, and Twitter (@UnityChronicler)

For all the latest news and insights into the universe of The Unity Chronicles, check out the official blog, Ex Nihilo, at http://theunitychronicles.blogspot.com

www.theunitychronicles.com

For Margaret Westwood, my mother,
with my eternal and heartfelt thanks.

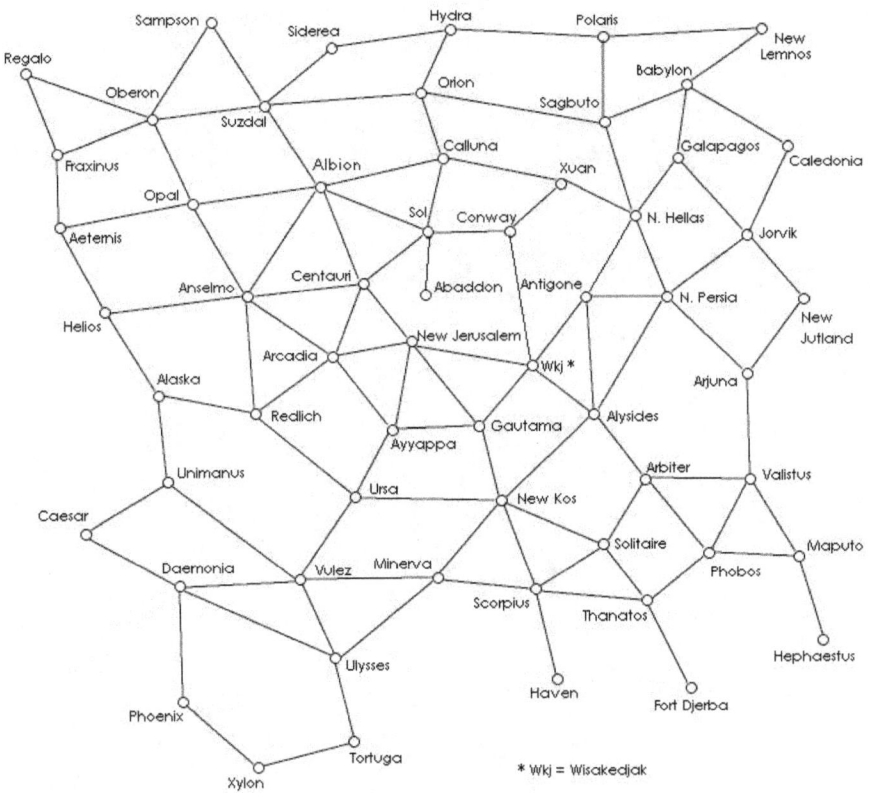

# Human colonies in the First Year of Unity

# Prologue

The silence was painful. Nobody wanted to be the one to point out that Max's ideas were turning from the unfeasible toward the absurd once more, because invariably that person would become the sole focus of his irrational attention for the next hour. Finally Neri threw herself on the proverbial conversational grenade.

"Nobody would buy that," she told him. "It wouldn't work. If they're looking for an excuse to centralise power in a supreme executive, they'll use a more mundane and believable one than cooking up a completely fictitious alien fleet."

"Not to mention a completely fictitious alien *race*," Cerydwyn offered bravely in support of Neri's point.

The silence fell once again as Max's attention - and derision - was quietly turned on the two women across the room from him. He might have been a handsome man, Neri found herself thinking, were it not for his insistence on growing an enormous hedge of a beard in honour of his hero from centuries past. If that was the fashion at that time, Neri was glad times had changed. It made him look at least half a dozen years older than he actually was.

"How can you be so blind?" Max finally asked, his voice quiet and affectedly melancholy. He had recently discarded his former affectations of the conspiracy-theory zealot anxious to convert all he met to his own personal view of the galaxy. In its place he had now adopted the somber mien of the fringe academic, certain of his views because of his greater expertise in the matter; disbelievers were not to be converted - how could they understand such lofty concepts? - but rather to be pitied. "This campaign against the independent outlier systems -"

"The pirates," Thom mock-helpfully supplied, the words pushing their way past the long, thin cigarette he held clamped between his thick lips.

"- is just the beginning," Max continued, pointedly not meeting Thom's gaze and instead focusing on educating the two women. "It is the nature of those in power to seek more.  It is obvious that the cooperation begun with this campaign -"

"Which is still nothing more than a rumour," Thom supplied cheerfully. This was enough to earn a burning look of derision from Max.

"If you are unwilling to even see what is plainly apparent in front of you," Max said, quietly and carefully, 'why are you a part of this group?"

Thom removed the cigarette from his mouth and leaned forward, the blithe smile dropping from his dark features. "Listen, Max. You might not appreciate the efforts I went to to *found* this little get-together of ours, but just remember whose house you're in - literally and figuratively. I created this group to provide a place for those of a like mind to gather and discuss the problems we and our brothers and sisters in the outlier systems face politically, socially, and logistically. I let you join us because you've got an impressive amount of academic expertise - but you're not here to take up our time with conspiracy theory and rumours blown out of all proportion. We are meant to be about real solutions for real problems."

Cerydwyn and Neri exchanged a look.  This was the first time in months that Thom had even spoken more than a few words at one of their meetings, and he had never confronted Max about his tendency toward conspiracy theories before.  Their usually-unflappable leader was starting to look positively angry.  Max, meanwhile, was either oblivious to Thom's anger, or only too glad to engage in an impassioned debate about the overall purpose of the group.

"You want to talk about real problems?" the bearded man began. "Try seven of the galaxy's most powerful corporations, many little better than sworn enemies of each other, combining their escort militias and private security forces into one huge amalgamated task force bound for the galactic south-west."

"Where are you getting your information?" Thom asked. "That sort of thing would be on the news, don't you think? It's not like people would fail to notice a fleet of that size just passing through their home system. It goes without saying that the media is controlled to a certain degree by the big corporations, but this is the sort of operation they couldn't hope to hide - they would cover it up by explaining it away. It would be in the news, but it would be called something else. It would be too big to simply disappear altogether!"

"That's because they haven't started yet" Max countered. Thom was stunned into momentary silence.

"Then how the fu-" he shouted, before getting a hold on his temper. "I repeat my previous question - where are you getting your information?" At this, Max seemed genuinely uncomfortable, running a long-fingered hand down his beard as he shifted posture in the low, deep sofa. He took a draught of coffee and stammered several times, searching for a suitable response.

"I'm not at liberty to say" he claimed, finally. Each of the three other members of the Progressive Policy Debate Forum immediately provided Max with their own personal sound of derision and howls of protest. He continued, raising his voice over the clamour. "But I assure you that my sources are reliable and indeed very close to the centre of all of this." The sceptical protests redoubled, and he had to shout to make himself heard. "You'll believe me when they burn Juliano Station! Then you'll know I'm right!" He stood and slammed his coffee cup down onto the wooden tabletop, the dregs leaping out to spatter into constellations across the pale surface. Stalking angrily to the door, he turned as if to offer a final rejoinder, but either came up short or thought better of it. The door swung shut quietly behind him.

"Bye, Max!" Thom called after him. "See you next week!"

# Part One
## Chapter 1

"Remind me again why you're in charge, *Sergeant*?" The voice came across the comm. channel, derision saturating it even through the hiss of static. Hieron sighed; he hadn't asked to be in charge and was probably even less pleased about it than those temporarily under his command.

"Because I have the most combat experience, Davik," Hieron replied calmly. "I'm sure it was nothing personal."

"Only reason you got the most combat experience is because you Arbiter Fuel guys love to shoot unprovoked," said a new voice, that of Blue Wing leader Vesta Fleck. Fleck was from Frontline Fuels, one of Arbiter's main market competitors and their opponents in more than one surreptitious dogfight. Hieron himself had destroyed more than a couple of Frontline escorts in his time.

"Oh that's rich coming from trigger-happy Frontline stickhand," came the response from Chao, one of Hieron's own squadron from Arbiter.

"Alright everyone, that's enough," Hieron told them. "We're here with a job to do, and we've been ordered to co-operate. Your employers all told you the same thing Arbiter told us - this sortie could be the start of something revolutionary."

"Sure, because stamping on pirates is a new idea" Fleck muttered.

"Stamping on them this hard is," he replied. "Check your formations and cut the chatter, people. Let's at least act like professionals." The dots on his scanner that showed him the position of the rest of the fleet started to adjust their distance from one another until they were as close to their designated positions as could be expected. For the first time since they had launched, Hieron allowed himself to hope that they could pull this off - that their differences could be put aside and the mission completed to everyone's satisfaction.

"Increase speed to four hundred emps and power your weaps" he ordered. "Shields to double front, scanners to one hundred clicks." He could see their target as a point of light in the distance, reflecting the system's solitary sun. So much like Sol, he thought to himself.

"Contact at ninety-eight clicks dead ahead," Chao reported. "Targets stationary, number uncertain."

"Looks like we're expected," Hieron noted. "Make sure to check for mines; sometimes they won't show up on scanners before one hundred clicks."

"We're not new at this, sir," Fleck reminded him. He was about to admonish her for that rebuke, but thought better of it: at least she had called him 'sir'.

"Targets at eighty clicks and closing at three hundred emps," Chao updated them. "No sign of any other contact. Maybe they just want to talk."

"Too late for that Chao," Hieron replied. "Talks with Juliano Station have repeatedly broken down and every one of our corporations have lost pilots and cargo to these pirates. Hence the choice of target. Ready missiles, and get me an accurate count on their numbers just as soon as you can."

"Aye sir."

He could almost make out the shape of the station at this range, and it may have been his imagination but he thought he could see a scatter of tiny specks surrounding it. Ships wouldn't be visible at this range, though, so it was either his imagination or something he'd have to bear in mind when they were closer to the target.

"Target reads at least eight distinct contacts," Chao reported. "Looks like mainly Godsforge Tercels."

"Godsforge huh?" said Eastoc, one of Davik's wingmen from the Titan Mining Group. "Any weaknesses you Godsforge boys and girls'd like to tell us about before we get stuck in here, as you've so kindly provided the opposition with their ships?"

"Fuck you Eastoc" came the response from Xina, the laconic leader of Black Wing. Godsforge Munitions had supplied the heavy bomber wing of the formation, which was bringing up the rear. Hieron had never seen an Osprey in combat before, and despite the tension of the situation he had to admit to himself that he was looking forward to witnessing their legendary firepower first-hand.

"Targets at twenty clicks, sir" Chao said. "They've adopted an offensive formation and have started toward us. Current velocity puts us nose-to-nose in less than thirty seconds."

"This is it," Hieron told them. "Everyone stay sharp, keep the comms open, and stay alive."

"Hard contact!" Bengt, the second Arbiter wingman, exclaimed. "Long-range missile bearing three five eight!"

"Evasive manoeuvres," ordered Hieron. "Red and Blue Wings break formation and engage. Green Wing fall back and protect the bombers." Each Wing leader acknowledged the order and Hieron dropped back on the throttle with the rest of his wing, watching the six remaining ships that formed Red and Blue Wings streak off toward the approaching defenders of Juliano Station.

"Confirm eight contacts Green leader," Fleck reported from several kilometres ahead. "Six Tercels and two Hornets. Nothing we can't handle. Son of a bitch!"

"Blue leader, report," Hieron called. "Fleck, come in."

"Quit your worrying Tomac, I'm still here. Close call with a Hornet, that's all. He's toast, but I lost Nyko."

"Green two, Green three, hold formation," Hieron ordered. "I'm going to assist. Black wing stay on target. Only break off your assault run if faced with heavy opposing fire."

"Understood, Green leader." Came Xina's reply. His wingmen likewise accepted the order, and he pushed the throttle forward to three hundred emps and joined the fray. His scanner showed several specks dipping and diving back and forth, weaving between and around each other. Smaller specks would periodically streak from one to another as missiles were exchanged.

"Bogey on my six," called Davik.

"Roger that Red leader, moving to intercept." Hieron threw his ship after the pirate Tercel and matched it turn for turn until he had a positive lock from his laser targeting systems. Pulling the trigger, he felt the familiar rush as hundreds of points of blue-lit death shot out of the cannons on either wing, streaking out toward the enemy's vessel and hitting home, draining the power to the rear shield. It wouldn't be long, he knew, before the power failed altogether and the lasers would start penetrating the hull. He had fought plenty of Tercels in his time.

"Get the fuck on with it Arby-boy, this guy isn't kidding around!" Davik seemed to be getting nervous, but with bright and comforting inevitability the laser shots eroded the pirate's hull, penetrating to the fuel tank and igniting the contents. The chain reaction was short but violent, and left nothing behind but drifting chunks of debris and human remains, the latter of which Hieron habitually did not look at too carefully.

"Patience is a virtue, Red leader," he said.

"So is punctuality," Davik growled back. "That bastard cooked my rear shield all to hell." He had already selected his next target and was closing fast, but still just out of laser range.

"Fall back and support the bombers," Hieron ordered. "I'll cover you."

"Fuck that shit, Arby-boy. I'm not about to sit back and let you fuellers take all the glory. Watch my six and I'll be just fine." His own cannons opened up on his target and he wove about as the pirate attempted to shake him. Hieron swore to himself and hung back, keeping Davik's fighter in view at all times. He wasn't used to insubordination, but then he wasn't used to command at all, so was unsure how to handle it.

He could hardly shoot Davik down for disobeying his order, could he? But either way it was setting a dangerous precedent.

"Green leader this is Black leader. Missile range in five seconds, we are beginning our initial run at the target."

"Roger that, Black leader," he responded, glad to be talking to someone who apparently had no trouble with his being in command. He restrained himself from further communication with Xina, afraid of compromising that particular command relationship. Glancing at the scanner, he caught the moment when twelve new contacts appeared ahead of the bombers, and looked to his left to see the heavy missiles streaking through the space between Black Wing and their target. They were a little over halfway when a second salvo was launched, twelve more points of light on a collision course with Juliano Station.

Hieron's mind imagined the *crump, crump* sound of the missiles hitting home as one wing of the space station was severed from the main body. The second volley slammed directly into the center of the station, crippling it almost entirely. The bombers made a close run past the expanding debris field ready to come around for a second and fatal pass. Just as they pulled past, a dozen missiles shot out from the still-intact upper section of the station, catching the Ospreys dead astern and completely unprepared. The rearmost pair were shattered by the assault and it must have been due to either precognition or tremendous reflexes on Xina's part that got her shields switched to double rear before the impact.

"Black leader, get the hell out of there!" he shouted into the comm, but she was already accelerating into a series of evasive manoeuvres before he had finished giving the order. He pulled his own fighter out of pursuit of one of the pirates. They needed to regroup and present a united front. "All wings, cover her ass and get a read on the fresh contact."

"You got it," Fleck acknowledged.

"Aye sir," came Chao's voice, tense from the change in their fortunes. No word from Davik.

"Red Leader, break off your attack and support Black leader."

"Thought I told you to fuck that shit, *sir*."

"You're going to get yourself, your men, and all of us killed, Red Leader. Break off your attack and regroup with the rest of the fleet."

"You have no idea what you're doing, do you?" Davik sneered through the comm link. "These fuckers aren't going to give us the room to regroup. We need to press the attack and fuck them before they fuck us." He killed the comm link, disappearing from Hieron's list of radio contacts.

"That idiot's going to get us all killed" Fleck muttered.

"That idiot's on his own now," Hieron told them. "And so are we. At the very least he's bought us a little time to regroup so everyone form up around the bomber and let's try to finish them off. Anyone get a read on those contacts?"

"Missile turrets on the upper section," Xina growled. "The sneaky bastards could have launched any time but chose their moment perfectly."

"Well they won't be doing the same this time so have your countermeasures prepped," Hieron instructed. "What's your shield status, Black Leader?"

"Switched to double-front, readout shows twenty percent. Might survive another hit but much more and I'm toast."

Hieron checked his scanner. The four remaining pirate vessels were being kept busy by Davik and his wingmen, but it was unlikely to stay that way for long. Equally unlikely were their chances of successfully escorting Xina on a final bombing run on the station - the missile turrets would destroy most of their fleet before they had a chance to return fire. The necessity of holding formation to protect her from direct hits would make them little more than sitting ducks for the pirates manning the turrets. Only one course of action presented itself to his mind, and it was risky to say the least.

"Blue wing, remain in formation and protect Black Leader at all costs. Her missiles are the only things that can get this job done properly. Green Wing form up on me; we're going to try to knock out those turrets to clear the way for the final missile run." A chorus of acknowledgments, with only a few hints of doubt. For the second time that day, he allowed himself to hope they might just beat the odds.

The three fighters of Green Wing formed their familiar wedge and sliced through the vacuum at full throttle. As the first volley of missiles were launched, the formation split and veered off on separate vectors, launching infrared countermeasures as they did so. With one exception, the missiles were drawn off by the ruse; the other had reacquired Bengt's heat signature and was tracking him as he ducked and rolled, trying to tax the missile's guidance system past breaking point.

Meanwhile Hieron and Chao had circled around to the rear of the station out of targeting range of the turrets and begun a short-range attack run, pulling their ships in a tight arc around the broken shell of the station and into laser range of the turrets. Opening up their cannons, they strafed the main bodies of the launchers, each fitted with dual launch pods. Two were shredded on their first run, their stocked ammunition providing the perfect catalyst. Hieron and Chao pulled back and once again entered the relatively safe area on the other side of the station.

Bengt, still unable to shake his missile, was evading as best he could when another salvo was launched, eight sparks of death bound straight for him. His pilot's instincts took over from his conscious mind and he maintained his top velocity as he flew head-on to meet them. At the last second, as his targeting computer screamed out his impending fiery death, he twisted the light, nimble ship into a corkscrew turn that sent him weaving between the missiles, and he tried not to notice how close one went past his cockpit's canopy. Unable to come about at one hundred and eighty degrees, their guidance systems simply gave in and they streaked off into the blackness of space.

Unfortunately his idea had only half-worked, as he noticed when the computer resumed warning him of the first missile doggedly tracking him and closing rapidly. He threw himself at the station at full speed, launching all his countermeasures in front of him. They shot out to pepper the surface of one of the missile launchers, and just as he and his ship were about to do the same he pulled up. The greater amount of heat being given off by the countermeasures was enough to confuse the missile's guidance into following the wrong signal, and another missile launcher was out of commission. Bengt joined the rest of Green Wing on the far side of the station as they prepared for another run.

"Damn it sergeant, we need support!" Davik's voice came back onto the comm channel. Hieron was in no mood to take risks on the behalf of the erstwhile leader of Red Wing, and he killed Davik's frequency.

"Are you insane Tomac?" Fleck's voice was incredulous. "He's been keeping those fighters busy for you this whole time and you're just going to let him whistle?"

"He disobeyed a direct order," Hieron replied calmly. "And therefore put every one of us, and the mission itself, in jeopardy. Combat effectiveness relies on a proper chain of command."

"Screw your chain of command!" She retorted. "Blue wing, on me. Red Wing, we're on our way to assist."

Hieron was fuming, his command crumbling around him as the three Frontline fighters sped over to join the fray. Fleck's remaining wingman had his career definitively ended by the Juliano missile launchers as they approached, and Hieron led Green Wing into another strafing run on the turrets. Two more were destroyed but the third scored a direct hit on Chao's underbelly, ripping his propulsion away and sending him into a spin. Hieron did not need to take a close look to know that his wingman was already dead.

"Tomac, we're in trouble here," Fleck's voice came over the comm. "It's just me and Davik left and we're up against a pair of aces in their Tercels. These guys are determined not to die." Hieron cursed in the privacy of his head.

"Bengt, get that last turret out of commission," he said aloud. "I'm going to assist Red and Blue."

"Roger that," came the reply.

Hieron turned his ship to join the ongoing dogfight not far away. Fleck was currently trying to pick one of the Tercels off from Davik's tail while simultaneously avoiding the one on hers. Hieron took off after the latter pirate, giving him something more pressing to think about than lining Blue Leader's propulsion up in his crosshairs. The pilot was talented; only a few of the shots Hieron took at her rear section found their mark as the ship bobbed and weaved on Fleck's tail.

"Blue Leader, this one's too good by half," Hieron told her. "We're going to need to do this together."

"No arguments here, Tomac," she replied, her voice strained as she puled her ship through a series of particularly strenuous turns.

"I need you to fly straight and then bank hard right. I'll be ready for it."

"You got it. Stand by." The pirate must have thought it was her lucky day, Hieron mused as Fleck straightened her line momentarily, bringing herself into a perfect line of fire. The pirate's cannons opened up immediately, but then the craft tilted and pulled hard right, the shots streaking harmlessly past her belly. Overconfident and frustrated in the pursuit of Fleck's ship, the pirate lunged after her, straight into Hieron's concentrated fire. It hit her forward section, cutting immediately through the weakened shields and into the cockpit. The threat was eliminated.

"Thanks Green Leader," Fleck's relieved voice sighed across the comm. "Looks like we make a pretty passable team after all."

"You may have a point there, Blue Leader" he replied cheerfully. "Now let's get on to relieving Davik of his troubles." He glanced down at the scanner, and his heart sank at what he saw. Fleck had apparently seen the same thing.

"Looks like the pirate beat us to it on that score," she said, her voice echoing his mood. The debris which was all that was that was left of Davik's craft was drifting silently half a kilometre away, and the engines of the pirate with whom he had been dicing were a vanishing spark in the distance. Its vector put it on a direct intercept course with the last remaining bomber. There was no way Hieron and Fleck could close the gap in time.

"Bengt, did you get-" Hieron began, but it seemed his wingman was as efficient as ever.

"Last missile turret offline, am in pursuit of your missing pirate. Closing at a rate of twenty metres per second. I might just make it. Shields to double front."

"We're on our way to assist" Hieron assured him, and with Fleck on his port wing he pushed the throttle to maximum. They began to close the gap behind the pirate's fighter but it was clear they weren't going to make it in time.

"Black Leader you have incoming bogey bearing zero two six, range six hundred clicks. Suggest getting the hell away from it. Fighter support inbound."

"You're the boss, Green Leader," Xina replied, calm and laconic.

"Green Two, range to target," Hieron barked.

"I'm right up his backside, Green Leader," Bengt replied. "Picking my shot." That couldn't be right. There was no way he could have closed the gap so fast unless -

"Green Two, evasive manoeuvres!" he ordered. But it was too late. The pirate had released a mine at low velocity, then powered away from the blast zone. In his headlong rush to intercept his target, the last of Hieron's wingmen from the Arbiter Fuel Corporation Escort Militia was either oblivious to the new threat or had no time to react. The only thing that saved him from being instantly vapourised was his reinforced frontal shielding. Nevertheless, the kinetic energy of the detonation threw him spinning off helplessly, making him an all-too-easy target for the pirate who had made a swift one-eighty turn and now bore down on him with both cannons blazing.

Bengt was long gone by the time Hieron and Fleck arrived, resuming the pursuit. They were careful not to fly directly on the pirate's tail and kept their shields at double-front. The gap was closing, slowly but surely.

"If we want to catch this guy off-guard," Xina suggested, "then I'll be more than willing to show him what an Osprey can do close-up."

"How confident are you?" Hieron asked, watching the scanner. Even with the bomber in full retreat, the Tercel would be able to take his shots at her before Hieron and Fleck could catch up. "Your shields are still low," he reminded her.

"I'll give him a surprise at least," she replied, "and if I come about you

13

two will be on him in no time."

"Alright, do it" he ordered.  The Osprey came about as rapidly as it could, just in time to light up the space between its nose and the pirate's with the laser shots from half a dozen cannons and turrets, eclipsing the minimal return fire.  A missile streaked out from its housing on one wing, and the pirate barely had time to react before the lasers drained its front shield and the missile detonated just rear of the canopy.  As a final coup de grace, the bomber closed with the stricken pirate and Xina used her focused magnetic tractor beam to reel it in like a stunned fish from a lake.  One missile gracefully ended the pirate's hopes of survival.

"Well I don't think either of us will be picking a fight with an Osprey any time soon," Fleck murmured as she and Hieron formed up on either wing of the heavy bomber.

"Status, Black Leader," Hieron requested.

"I've had worse, Green Leader," she replied.  "Micro-fracture in the hull from that last little exchange.  My suit's sealed and I've got oxygen, but I can't put it through hyperspace until I get this patched up." Hieron knew as well as she did that such a repair was unlikely to say the least, given their current location.  Any help sent from their base in the next system would take longer to get back to her than she had left; the oxygen would last maybe twelve hours.

"Understood, Black Leader," he said.  "Care to help us finish off this godforsaken mission?"

"My missiles are yours to command, sir."

So the three remaining corporate escort ships set off back toward their half-stricken target, surrounded by its own debris field, and oversaw its final demolition.  The mission was complete, and as far as Hieron was able to tell, there had been no hostile survivors.  Juliano Station and its independent, lawless, scavenging population would trouble the galaxy's major corporations no longer.

# Chapter 2

Kiah Sicarius was impatient. This described both his general disposition and his mood at the current moment, as he paced back and forth on the spotlessly gleaming white tiles. His thin legs carried him across the floor in a manner reminiscent of an insect, or a large bird, and the latter image was only enhanced by his shock of white curls contrasting sharply with his young features.

Finally, the door outside of which he was pacing slid open silently and the figure of Langton Parnett loomed out. Even in this room with its high ceilings and doorways to match, Parnett habitually ducked through the archways as very tall men become used to doing. He looked down his long nose at the young man who had ceased his pacing and approached him.

"They're back," he rumbled, and ducked back through the doorway. The white-haired man followed him through, entering a long room dominated by the central conference table and several very large wall charts. Eight other people including Parnett turned to greet their guest, who for his part was in no mood for pleasantries.

"What have you heard?" he asked the collection of VIPs in general. It was Balfour, the rotund British CEO of Galactic Agriculture, who answered him.

"The mission was a success, Sicarius. Juliano Station has been destroyed and all hostiles neutralised."

"What of the task force?" he demanded, the colour flooding his face as he grew frustrated at having to dig for the answers he sought.

15

Balfour dropped his gaze and muttered something incomprehensible under his breath. Kiah's gaze settled instead on Venk, the thin, shrill head of Liberty Shipyards of New York. Her pretentious accent would begin to crumble under pressure, Kiah had discovered, revealing her roots in the rougher parts of Brooklyn.

"Both Green and Blue leaders have reported in," she told him. "But from what they tell us, they were the only survivors." Kiah stood at the head of the long table, fixing Ms Venk with a long, flat stare. His cheeks were flushed and his hands formed fists on the tabletop. He knew how intimidating people found him to be at times; he had reasoned that it was something to do with his unusual appearance and quick temper. He tried to disguise his relief at Hieron's survival so as to better focus on the disastrous nature of the rest of the outcome. He made sure to control his voice; shouting tended to make people believe that the worst was over, whereas quiet, clearly-restrained rage tended to hint at greater fireworks to come.

"Two survivors" he stated with measured words. "From a task force of twelve. Ten pilots - good pilots, volunteers I must remind you - have lost their lives from this endeavour. Need I remind you all of the meetings we had preceding this mission? Of the warnings you were given that victory would rest on staging a well-planned, well-supplied sortie against a minor but significant target? Of the protests that the minuscule resources you were willing to commit would be barely adequate?"

"Nevertheless the strike was approved unanimously-" Dang Zhou interjected, cutting himself short as Kiah met his eyes. Dang Zhou was an arrogant, self-obsessed moron whose inclusion in the group was purely down to his status as the current CEO of Godsforge Munitions. Kiah had very little time for him, and the look he was directing at the man suggested strongly that what little there was was rapidly running out.

"Unanimously, under protest," Kiah reminded him. "I seem to recall that our illustrious military adviser was vocally opposed to the plan as it stood, and yet like myself was conveniently not accorded a vote. Am I correct, General?" He addressed the tall, quiet figure sitting unobtrusively in the shadows of the corner.

"You are correct, Mr Sicarius" she replied, leaning forward and allowing the overhead lighting to illuminate her sharp but delicate, barely-lined features.  General Manda Leetman had been called in to advise the group on the military aspects of their business, something she was more than qualified to do, being the former Chief of Staff for the Air Force of the Earth States Commonwealth.  It was painfully clear at times how much of a step down she considered her current position.  "Considering the intelligence reports we had received regarding the target, I recall suggesting a sortie of at least twenty ships.  As for the morale issues, I distinctly remember advising that the sortie teams be put through team-building exercises and training programs.  What I believe happened was that they were allowed to meet once before the mission."

"With all due respect, General" Dang Zhou replied,  "You make it sound as if they simply had lunch together, when in fact they spent an entire day in the mission briefing, which included certain team-building activities."

"Unless you started shooting at them and forced them to co-operate in a truly life-threatening situation, it was not even slightly sufficient preparation" she retorted witheringly.

The door slid open again and a suited official entered, whispered something to Langton Parnett, and left again.  He in turn cast his lofty gaze around the room.  "The two pilots have just docked," he informed them.  "They're on their way here now."

- - - - -

Kiah remembered seeing pictures of churches from the twentieth century and before, and it was little wonder to him that the religion practised within those ornate, archaic walls became as outdated as the buildings themselves.  Even the attempts at modernisation saw only the creation of monstrous mockeries of the former architecture in steel and glass; as with matters of policy, it was their stubborn unyielding nature that led to their obsolescence.

In stark contrast to the ornate, gold-enamelled décor of the past, the room in which he now stood was a study in comfort and simplicity. two deep, long, ruby red couches occupied the entire lengths of two walls, with two dark wood tables set before each.  The ceiling was relatively low, and housed several spotlights which could be adjusted to suit the mood.  It was the sort of room in which one had friendly discussions with people of a like mind, and spoke of everything from the weather to politics, and the politics of weather. The only clue that it was a place of religious significance was the large central insignia on the carpet.

The small wooden door set in the far wall swung open, making a peaceful whisper on the thick carpet as it did so. The man revealed standing on the other side was a slight, hook-nosed man in his twilight years. Nevertheless, he wore a spotless business suit of the highest quality, and stood straight despite his age. He beckoned to the young white-haired man, and they both walked through the well-lit corridors until they reached his office. He closed the door behind them and bade Kiah to sit. As always when in the presence of the Father, Kiah did his best to ignore the young girl sat unobtrusively in the corner of the room. It was customary for the Primus to have a young acolyte study him for the entirety of the acolyte's life, so that by the time the Primus was finally called on to take his final rest, there would be a suitable candidate ready to replace him.

"Tell me everything, my young friend," the old man requested as he settled into his high-backed, well-cushioned reclining chair. "Leave nothing unsaid." Kiah settled himself in the nearby chair which was only slightly less luxurious than the other, treating himself to a look around the office as he did so. It was only a small room, certainly, but more closely resembled a lounge than the personal private office of the head of the single largest religion in the galaxy. But then, that was part of the point.

"As I told you, Father," Kiah began, "the corporation heads proved reluctant to co-operate on anything more than a token level. It took a great deal of persuasion to reach the point at which a sortie was feasible. Even then, General Leetman was insistent that the pilots needed further training to hone them into a single unit; unfortunately the heads would not be moved and we were forced to proceed with what we had. The two factors that let us down the most, aside from the constrained resources, were a lack of trust, and poor intelligence regarding the Station's defensive capabilities."

Kiah continued to relate the stages of the battle as they had been told to him by Hieron and Vesta Fleck, and later verified by examination of their flight recorders. The old man frowned mightily, his bushy eyebrows meeting in a dark grey V in the middle of his forehead, when he told him of Davik's insubordination. He even looked a little excited when Green Wing were making their strafing runs against the missile turrets, and shed a compassionate tear with every pilot who passed - including the pirates.

Kiah then moved on to the proceedings of the debriefing meeting which had followed the two pilots' return. "We decided that, despite the heavy losses incurred, the mission was broadly successful. After all, the objective had been completed, and there was evidence that at least some of the traditional enmity between the factions had been eroded. In fact, the two pilots who returned had been bitter rivals prior to the mission, working as they do for two different fuel corporations; yet after this trial by fire they are, if not trusting allies, at least open to the idea of cooperation. She has difficulty following his orders, but only when they clash with what she herself considers to be the best course of action. There are seeds of alliance there which may well be made to flourish in the correct circumstances."

"And what, my dear boy, are we doing to ensure that those circumstances come to pass?" the old man asked.

"The next stage of the campaign has been approved, but the exact logistics are still being discussed. What has so far been confirmed is that the target will be the substantial privateer base in the northern forests of Korpi, in the Xylon system; all seven of the corporations will be required to provide a significant portion of the assault force; this assault force will be trained for a period of two weeks in whatever way General Leetman deems necessary. It is likely that this sortie will require significant use of ground forces, though we are exploring alternatives due to the high risks and obvious drawbacks of such a tactic."

"What of Hieron?" Kiah smiled at this question, a thin, subtle line spreading across his sharp features.

"Hieron Tomac is about to receive two very unwelcome pieces of news, Father."

- - - - -

"*Fired?*" Hieron asked, incredulously and loudly. He stood before the desk of his CEO at Arbiter Fuel Corp, Langton Parnett, who was sat in his swiveling leather chair looking increasingly uncomfortable at having to deal with this particular interaction. Parnett was not a people person at the best of times, and this was far from qualifying for that category.

"I assure you, Tomac, it is a mere f-formality" Parnett rumbled awkwardly. "You are just being asked to step down from your position within the Arbiter Fuel Corporation Escort Militia and assume a command role within our organisation. It is thought that it would help remove some of the enmity and trust issues within the alliance's military assets if the leader of the mission does not belong to any one of the constituent factions." Hieron stared at him unblinking for a few moments, marshalling his response.

"First of all, sir," he began, choosing his words carefully, "nobody in their right mind is going to buy such a superficial distinction. I'm an Arbiter pilot and everyone knows it. Secondly, how do I take an official position within an organisation that does not technically, legally, or financially exist? Which brings me to my final and most important point. Who is going to pay me?"

"We are a collection of the most powerful, and indeed wealthy corporations in the galaxy, Tomac," Parnett reminded him. "We would have absolutely no problem in providing you with suitable compensation for your efforts, and of course It goes without saying that if this experiment in cooperation does not go according to plan, then you will be reinstated at your current level or higher in the Militia. As for the charge of superficiality, well that I can't deny; it certainly wasn't my idea. But I was outvoted, so here we are. At the very least it can hardly make things worse."

"Well I suppose the only other choice I have is to tell you to go to Hell," Hieron mused. "But I'm not sure I want to contemplate what a group of powerful corporations would do to someone who just walked away from them with knowledge of their very secret alliance. So sign me up." He sat resignedly into the chair opposite Parnett, when something occurred to him. "You mentioned two things," he said, freshly apprehensive. "When you brought me in here you said you had two things to tell me. Please say you gave me the bad news first."

"That depends on your perspective, I suppose," Parnett murmured, seemingly half to himself. "The other thing I had to tell you is regarding the current assault plan. While there are still many areas of the mission that remain fluid, it is certain that we will be sending a capital ship along; probably a Godsforge Valkyrie. It will provide a forward command center and tactical weapons platform which will be vital to the success of the mission." Parnett paused, and shifted uncomfortably in his seat. Hieron interpreted this as a prelude to the next portion of bad news, and he was not disappointed. "You are to command the Valkyrie."

"No," he said immediately. "I am a pilot, Mr Parnett, not a cruiser captain. Aside from the fact I have no experience on the bridge of something that big, I have substantial experience on the stick of a fighter. It's a stupid idea, sir, forgive me for saying so; you'll have a weak command and a large gap in the fighter escort that I should be filling."

"I appreciate your position," Parnett replied quietly, "and I'll omit the word 'stupid' when I recount this to my colleagues. But I am afraid this is a condition upon which they have insisted, Sicarius in particular. He is a hard man to turn down." Hieron wondered how a man so socially awkward and afraid of conflict had ever risen to be CEO of arguably the galaxy's biggest supplier of fuel. "They want you in a position to direct the battle," Parnett continued, at once seemingly desperate to talk him around and yet reluctant to argue his point. "They were apparently quite impressed by your tactical process during the assault on Juliano. And of course you would be safer on the bridge of a Valkyrie than anywhere else on the field." He seemed not to grasp the irony of appealing to a fighter pilot's sense of safety and self-preservation.

"Let me guess," Hieron said, flatly. "This is as much of a choice as the getting fired part, is it?"

"I'm afraid so," Parnett replied, and seemed genuinely remorseful; this was probably attributable more to the fact that he disliked giving bad news than genuine regret about Hieron's situation.

"We'll see about that," Hieron declared as he stood to leave. "I can be just as stubborn as those bastards if I choose."

"A compromise would be better than simply disagreeing, don't you think?" Parnett called after him as he reached the door. Hieron listened to what the tall, awkward man had to say, and it became clear to him then how his former CEO had reached the lofty station he had.

- - - - -

The next day was spent in training, Hieron being given instruction in how to sit and give orders to manoeuvre the ship instead of simply moving a stick. It still felt unnatural to him, though the experience was made more pleasant by the company of his instructor - a diminutive young technician with Godsforge Munitions named Klaira. He wondered a number of times whether the choice of having her instruct him had been made deliberately to improve his mood, but he dismissed the thought each time out of a fervent wish that his employers were not that devious.

The first thing they had done upon entering the hangar containing the Valkyrie he would be commanding was undertake an inspection of the vessel both external and internal; this satisfied both the need for such an inspection prior to deployment, and for her new captain to familiarise himself with the kind of ship he would be controlling. Once or twice he allowed himself to inappropriately enjoy the sight of Klaira climbing the steps before him.

The ship's name, he was told, was *Hariasa*. He was unsure where they had come up with a name like that, but it seemed to suit her. She was huge, of course, with a crew of seventy-two, but had a grace to her features that reminded Hieron of some of the smaller fighters. Indeed, Klaira informed him that it was the most manoeuvrable ship of its size currently in operation. Somehow, that piece of information made him feel a little more comfortable with the idea of captaining her.

What made him less comfortable was the woman who was to be his second in command, a harsh woman with a permanent sour look on her face. It was only later that Hieron discovered the reason for her perpetual bad mood, and for the time being it was just a minor annoyance. He was quite used to the attitudes of some of the other personnel from rival corporations, and although Arbiter and Godsforge had never been enemies, there was significant rivalry between their respective security forces.

Thankfully Klaira displayed none of that hostility as she explained the ship's systems to him, patiently at times and briefly at others, when the systems were essentially enlargements of what he was already used to. Like most career technicians he had known, she had an inexhaustible enthusiasm for her work and was clearly having far more fun than him. Finally they visited the bridge, and he got his first look at what was to be his chair, from which he would control the most important aspects of operating the *Hariasa*, and direct the battle as a whole. He disliked it intensely.

It sat high at the rear of the bridge, so high in fact that there was a step up to reach it. It was high-backed and far more comfortable-looking than any of the other furniture he had seen on board, and it was surrounded by a hundred complex-looking dials and gadgets that he knew he would have no hope of recognising as analogous to the controls of his cockpit. He turned to Klaira.

"So how many of those controls will I actually need when I'm commanding this thing?" he asked her, hoping for a clear, simple response. He should have known better.

"Well that depends entirely on your command style, sir," she replied cheerfully, and he knew what was coming next. "You see, it's all set up so that no matter what system you would prefer to have control over, the chair can meet your needs. The dials at the rear of each arm control the displays you see at the other end, so if you wanted you could have direct control over comms on your left hand and weapons on the right, or if you wanted more specific control of the weapons you can split those commands into distinct groups so that you control the targeting subroutines - such as priority lists for the auto-target or even manual crosshairs targeting like you'd be used to - on your right hand while controlling loading or launching or whatever on your left. Or if you -" Hieron held up his hand.

"OK Lieutenant," he smiled. "I get the picture. What I should have asked was, is there anything there that is absolutely necessary for me to do my job effectively that I cannot do elsewhere?" She thought for a moment.

"No, sir. The majority of the systems there are overrides - you would essentially be taking control of the weapons, for example, away from the weapons officer. Likewise with navigation, comms and the rest."

"So everything I can do with the gadgets in the chair, I can do by giving verbal orders. Yes?"

"Yes" she nodded.

"Good" he said. "Because I absolutely have no intention of going anywhere near that thing."

- - - - -

The next six days consisted of a strange combination of battle drills, live fire exercises, and team building activities. The latter eventually struck Hieron as a true stroke of genius; the activities themselves in no way seemed to promote the cohesion of the group, and yet the pilots and crew from the various factions began to bond - over what a boring, hideous waste of their time it was.

The numbers involved in the next sortie were to be substantially greater than the previous one, with at least five ships contributed by each of the seven corporations. Additionally there were the ground forces, fifty hired mercenaries who looked for the most part more like a mob of vigilantes than highly-skilled elite special forces. Idly Hieron wondered how easy it would be, in the icy forests of Korpi, to tell which were the pirates and which were the mercenaries. It was of course quite possible that these hired forces were simply pirates from another area of the galaxy, only too glad to remove some competition. Needless to say, Hieron was glad to be remaining in the relative safety of the planet's orbit for the duration.

He was crossing the main hangar toward the *Hariasa* around noon on the final day of preparation when he spotted his soon-to-be second in command walking in the same direction; if they continued as they were, they would board at the same time and he would be forced to endure her stony silence every step of the way to the bridge. Painfully aware of how childish it was, he hurriedly ducked behind a nearby console before she could see him, nearly tripping over a technician's legs as he did so. He muttered an apology and was met with a cheerful, familiar face emerging from underneath the console.

"Well fancy meeting you here, sir," Klaira greeted him happily. "Was there something you needed?"

"Um," he began, trying to think of a convincing reason for him to be hiding behind a console. Damn it, he wasn't even sure what this console was meant to be for. Honesty, then. "Avoiding someone," he admitted quietly.

"Oh," was her interested and sympathetic response as she climbed out from underneath the console and knelt to look across toward the ship. "You're hiding from Teera Dent?" she asked, slightly incredulous. "Why?"

"Well this may sound paranoid" he explained reluctantly, "but I think she hates me. Every time I'm with her she hardly looks at me except to glare, and what few words she says to me purely out of necessity are positively filled with venom. Are you telling me that she's not like this with everyone? It's just me?"

"Well she does have good reason of course," Klaira informed him. "You basically stole her ship."

"I did what?" he asked, disbelieving. "How does that make even the remotest sense?" Klaira seemed slightly taken aback by his reaction.

"The *Hariasa* is Dent's command," she explained patiently. "When the heads took it away from her and gave it to you, it may have upset her a little." She cocked her head to one side in curiosity. "So they didn't tell you that your new second in command used to captain the ship you'll be flying?"

"That's correct," he muttered through gritted teeth. She shook her head in amused disbelief.

"They weren't kidding when they lectured us on trust issues were they?"

"No," he replied. "They certainly were not."

He thanked her for the information and continued on to board the *Hariasa*, striding confidently now along the corridors which only a week ago had seemed so dauntingly labyrinthine. Presently he emerged onto the bridge and beckoned Dent over to one side, hoping to nip this issue in the bud before the mission began, lest it cause problems when they are less easily dealt with.

"Captain Dent, let me first of all apologise for the way in which you were temporarily relieved of your command. I have only just recently been informed of the state of affairs myself, or I would have sought you out earlier. Please understand that I did not request command of your ship, but those in higher places would have it no other way. As far as I am concerned, this is still your ship; I'm just here to provide the tactical overview of the mission and coordinate the assault." She was staring at him impassively, which was almost as unnerving as the glaring to which he had been subjected previously. He let the gap in the conversation grow, hoping that she would respond in some way. Finally she relented.

"Look, Mister Tomac, I appreciate that you didn't ask for this any more than I did, but I'm sure you can understand that it is hard for a captain to be separated from her command in any way - be it substantial or symbolic. The reason I know you will be able to relate to this is sitting in my cargo bay taking up the space normally reserved for the emergency rations." She was referring to Parnett's master stroke of compromise; though in command of the *Hariasa*, Hieron had been permitted to bring his own fighter along with him, provided it took up no space in the fighter bay. He would not be permitted to use it except in the most dire of emergencies, but he found it comforting to know it was there, not far away from him, at all times. "You're not even going to get to fly the thing," Dent continued, "and yet you couldn't bear to be parted from it. Imagine how you felt when they told you you wouldn't be in that ship tomorrow, then imagine they told you someone else would be flying it instead, and you'll understand why you're not my favourite person right now." She was right.

He left the bridge again and headed for the briefing room. It was only a few hours before the final briefing, and he wanted to look over some more notes. On his way back across the hangar, he overheard some raised voices coming from a corner busy with large metal packing crates. As he drew closer, he discerned that there were at least twelve people having a loud and unfriendly difference of opinion. He raised himself quietly onto one of the crates to observe, making sure he remained unseen as he did so.

The people before him represented six of the seven corporations, the only one unrepresented being his former employers, Arbiter Fuel. Hieron deduced that they were all Hornet crews, two-man gunboats that did not feature in the fleets of the Arbiter Escort Militia. Perhaps they had just returned from a training sortie, he thought.

"We are so fucked," opined one young woman wearing the insignia of Galactic Agriculture. "A whole fleet of us and we're nothing but enemies."

"Shit, Emin, haven't you seen enough in the last few days to realise we're on the same side now?" This was spoken by a man of perhaps forty years, in the employ of Tranquility Aerospace, the main competitor for Godsforge on the military shipyards market. It was Tranquility Aerospace who produced the Hornet.

"That's awful short-sighted of you" drawled a Texan working for Liberty Shipyards. "Considerin' just yesterday I got word a Tranq squadron passin' through Galapagos failed to assist a Carter Tech convoy that got itself caught in a privateer ambush."

"Rumours ain't worth the paper they ain't printed on, Tex" declared a Cockney girl who looked to be barely out of her teens. Hieron couldn't make out her insignia from where he sat, but she was stood with the Tranquility Aerospace pilot.

"You're all missing the big picture here," boomed the voice of a giant from Godsforge Munitions. "Even if we're all on the same side, who's to say it's the right side? I don't know about you, but I've got family out in the fringe colonies, and I'm starting to get concerned about this whole campaign and where we might be headed."

"I'd be interested to know," Hieron interjected, immediately demanding their full and surprised attention as they saw him stood above them on the crate, "how many of you, by show of hands, have known someone who has been killed by a pirate." A few hands shot up, followed, in some cases reluctantly, by all the others. Hieron jumped down to their level and addressed them eye-to-eye. "Nobody wants to deny people the right to do as they wish. That's not what this cooperative venture is about. It's about making the galaxy a safer place for everyone, so that more people are able to make that same move to the outlier colonies in search of a fresh start." Emin interrupted him.

"All very nice, but I'd bet money that I could get just as many hands in the air by asking how many people have lost comrades to rival corporations." This met with a muted chorus of agreement from many of the others.

"It's true that our employers have a history of rivalry, and sometimes even outright enmity. But the difference between us and the privateers out there is that we have listened to reason, and submitted to diplomacy. Instead of settling our differences at the end of a laser cannon, we have done it over the conference table. I have lost count of how many times we have appealed to the privateers' sense of reason, and begged them for diplomacy. I myself once escorted an unarmed transport into the eastern fringe systems to deliver a harmless diplomat to an independent space station. The transport was sabotaged and lost with all hands, while the blast destroyed two of our escort fighters." He paused, not for effect but because his voice was starting to crack. His best friend had been one of those lost on that mission, and barely a day went by when he failed to feel his loss as if it had been mere hours ago.

"We have tried talking," he continued finally. "We have tried reasoning with them. We have all of us tried to take on the pirates as a part of sorties for our separate employers. Everything we have done so far has failed - except this. Less than a week ago, I commanded a small force from four different corporations, and together we destroyed a base of piracy that has been a thorn in the side of every military and commercial enterprise in the galactic south west for the past ten years. Now, it's still early days. This mission of ours tomorrow will only be the second cooperative sortie of its kind in recent history. But we are better equipped, better trained, and better informed than last time - and all we have to do is trust one another. Make no mistake - this is not going to be easy. But it is the only way to ensure the future safety of the outlier colonies."

A few hundred metres away, in a small room cluttered with monitors, Kiah Sicarius watched the scene in the hangar unfold with great curiosity and satisfaction. He turned to Langton Parnett who stooped beside him, and smiled.

"This is why we needed your man, Mr Parnett," he told the Arbiter CEO. "He is simply the perfect candidate to lead this whole endeavour."

"The perfect figurehead, you mean," Parnett corrected him.

"That's what I said," Kiah smiled back.

# Chapter 3

Sending a large and varied fleet through hyperspace was a logistical nightmare, as Hieron was discovering. He did not pretend to understand the physics behind the technology - his eyes had glazed over with every other pilot's during that particular briefing - but the implications were only too apparent. From what he understood, mass was the problem; an object travelling through hyperspace travelled much faster the less massive it was, so a fighter could make any given jump in significantly less time than a cruiser making the same jump. In practical terms this meant that getting a fleet to the same point at the same time, when that fleet comprised ships of at least three different sizes, required different launch times for each type of ship.

Then there was the problem of ensuring that none of the ships collided with each other when emerging into normal space at the destination. Holding formation in hyperspace simply wasn't feasible, apparently; he recalled some equations with worrying large numbers which, he was told, meant that even the most infinitesimally small deviation in course at the point of origin could result in emerging many thousands of kilometres away from the target. Particularly long jumps were discouraged for this very reason - nobody wanted to emerge from hyperspace in the middle of a star.

Part of the problem would be solved by having all of the TA-69 Hornets loaded into the two fighter bays aboard the *Hariasa*, thus reducing the number of different ships to just two - the smaller LS-72s, and the *Hariasa* herself. From what little he had gleaned from his brief meetings with the corporate heads, there had been an attempt to persuade Dang Zhou of Godsforge Munitions to provide another Valkyrie-class cruiser in which to carry the LS-72s, but he had been adamant that such a commitment would need to be matched by a similar increase in those of his counterparts. This was, it seemed, not an option.

The first real surprise of the briefing for Hieron was when the plan for deploying the ground troops was revealed. Normally it would be a job for several dropships, housed in the *Hariasa*'s fighter bays; but as these were saturated with Hornets, someone had come up with a rather creative alternative. Hieron was dubious about it to say the least.

"Escape pods?" he asked, genuinely thinking he had misheard.

"That's correct," Parnett assured him. "It seems they have state of the art guidance systems installed, meaning they can be placed with precision to within a few metres from high orbit."

"We conducted a few preliminary tests of such a usage of the systems when they were in the final stages of the design process," the founder of Carter Technologies supplied. "The main problem appeared to be disorientation on the part of the occupant, but we're confident that that particular deficiency has been more or less overcome."

"Putting aside for a moment exactly what you mean by 'more or less'," Hieron replied, "that was not my primary concern about this plan. I have to admit that I'm having a hard time getting past the fact that we're planning to use the escape pods for something other than evacuating the ship. What exactly are we supposed to do if the *Hariasa* is lost?"

"We do not foresee that circumstance arising," Miles Balfour assured him. "With the intelligence we have available, we have calculated that the odds of the flagship being sufficiently damaged to necessitate evacuation are negligible."

"Even in that unlikely event," Ms Venk added in her nasal bureaucrat's voice, "enough escape pods will remain so that the majority of the crew of the cruiser would be saved."

"Well as long as a majority survive, what could be wrong?" Hieron muttered to himself. "What about that General of yours - Leetman was it? Did she sign off on this plan?" His question was met with a hesitant silence before the strong, arrogant voice of Dang Zhou assaulted the air.

"The General was made to accept the practicalities of the situation. Once we had explained the logistics to her, she agreed that the plan we have before us now is the best possible allocation of our resources."

"She said that?" he asked. Most of the corporate heads nodded in agreement, with one or two uncertain exceptions. "Is that why she isn't here now? Because she felt confident in having you seven pompous fools represent her views in an honest and straightforward way?"

"Young man, do you have any idea who you're talkin' to?" demanded Wareck Gendson, his red moustache bristling indignantly. Hieron turned to look him straight in the eye.

"Right now I'm talking to the arrogant son of a bitch in charge of Frontline Fuels, the main competitor of Arbiter, my former employer. I also seem to be talking to a room full of amateur military experts whose only experience of combat is the backstabbing that got them where they are today. You cannot fight a battle with numbers on a page, probabilities and percentage loss estimates. A majority survival for a lost ship is *not* perfectly acceptable when you are the ones responsible for taking away their escape pods!" He slammed his fist on the table to punctuate his last sentence. It was a few moments before anyone else spoke.

"Mr Tomac," came the soft voice of Ari Zack, the hereditary head of Tranquility Aerospace. "We appreciate your perspective on these matters, but do please remember that you are the commander of the task force, not a member of, or adviser to, this policy forum." She rose, and ushered him toward the door. "This briefing is complete; you will be provided with all the necessary data you will need to pass on our orders to the task force." The door shut behind him, and Zack returned to her seat.

"Anyone else think it'd be easier to replace that insubordinate fuck?" Grendson asked the group.

"I don't see why not," Dang Zhou commented. "Any one of our commanders would be more than a match for the position, and I guarantee that anyone from Godsforge would be far more respectful in his dealings with us."

"Out of interest," Balfour began, "has anyone thought of the other side of the coin of this 'civilian' commander situation? I know it's intended to provide a direct link, from all of us as a unit, to the troops; but from the troops' perspective there's just this chap, with no official rank any more, who is therefore technically ranked beneath them all - even the cadets and technicians - and yet who is commanding the entire operation? Will they follow his orders at all?"

"Well what do you suggest, Balfour?" asked Larrel Carter, leaning forward and steepling his fingers thoughtfully. Balfour looked left and right at his rivals and compatriots, each face containing both aspects.

"Why not Leetman?" he suggested. "She's a General, so has the rank; she's in our pay, so she has the loyalty; and she is not associated with any of our militia or security forces."

"Leetman detests us," Asta Venk reminded them all.

"And yet she still does as we tell her," Carter noted. "If she truly had no regard for us or this venture, she would have excused herself from our service long ago." There was a general murmured chorus of agreement.

"Tomac stays," a quiet but firm voice came from the corner of the room, and they all turned to see Kiah Sicarius sat unobtrusively in comfortable chair, looking as if he had been there all along. Not one of them was able to say for certain that he had not. "He is the best man for the job, and indeed the only man for the job. Leetman is doing fine where she is, and no other candidate you could raise would meet all the necessary criteria. If nothing else, the troops will want a commander who has been in charge from the beginning - continuity you see."

"My Vesta Fleck commanded a wing in the assault on Juliano Station" Grendson reminded him. "She may not have been in command, but at least she was there, and survived." Kiah nodded thoughtfully, appearing to genuinely consider the possibility.

"Fleck would be a worthy choice indeed," he conceded. "An accomplished pilot and leader with, as you so rightly point out, the experience in cooperative combat that we require. However, she is the embodiment of this fleet's problems with trust; even in the previous mission, she failed to trust her commander enough to follow every order she was given, and the transcript of the comm traffic suggests an attitude of insubordination that is distasteful in the mess hall, and positively unacceptable in a combat situation. No, I do not think Vesta Fleck is a sensible choice." He rose from his chair, walking slowly along the length of the table. Each person shifted uncomfortably as he passed. "Tomac is the only candidate for this position," he told them. "And his most notable qualification is this, ladies and gentlemen."

As he spoke, a video was projected holographically from the centre of the table. They all watched as Hieron addressed the Hornet pilots, allaying their fears and quashing what could have been a potential mutiny. Not one failed to note the way the pilots looked at him come the end of the recording. Trust was evident even in the poor-quality, pixellated faces. Kiah smiled. "He believes in this venture, my friends. He knows why it is necessary, and why it can work. Why it *must* work." As abruptly as he had - presumably - arrived, Kiah disappeared out of the conference room door.

"Remind me why we need *him*?" Wareck Grendson grumbled. "He makes me uneasy."

"We need him," replied Langton Parnett "because he represents the official and unofficial blessings of the Church. Without him, the Primus withdraws his funding, and more importantly his future public support. When we finally let people know what we're doing out here, we're going to need all the support we can get. There's nobody in a better position than the Primus to supply what we need. You want to do without Sicarius, you'd best think of a way we can do without the Church of Intentionality." His statement was met by silence.

- - - - -

*I must be fucking mad,* Hari Selk thought to himself as he checked the fixtures on his harness. The single bulb above his head was providing just enough light for him to see by, and he wasted no time in checking, double-checking, and re-checking his equipment, particularly the mass of cables and straps that secured him to the walls. The one thing he did not dare to check was the quick-release mechanism - it had taken him the better part of twenty minutes to strap himself into this rig and he was damned if he was going to go through that all over again.

The display screen in front of him had a relatively simple interface, which currently showed the time remaining until his escape pod, along with the forty-nine others containing his mercenary comrades, would be jettisoned into the atmosphere of the planet Korpi. The guided descent would take him to within two kilometres of the target, with an RV half way. One good thing about the escape pod insertion, they had been told, was that it would be very unlikely for them to be hit by anti-air artillery. As that had been the first mention of triple-A, the briefing had not filled him with confidence.

Still, from everything they were saying, this should be a walk in the park. To call their opponents pirates would be to imply even some loose organisational structure, which would apparently be massively disingenuous. What they truly faced was a small number of people who scraped a living on this backwater colony by ambushing trade lanes and taking what they needed by sheer force of arms. Selk had seen more than enough action to know that force of arms only worked well against poorly trained targets. Pit those same people against just a few well-trained, well-provisioned men - even just one fifth of their number - and numbers, gutsiness, and the size of their weapons would count for very little indeed.

This thought put a smile on Selk's face. It was a batshit crazy mission, sure, but it was a mission. It was a chance to get his blood running, his adrenaline pumping, his breath racing. It was a chance to put his hard-won skills to the test once again, and feel like he was a part of something wonderful. A military unit, even a mercenary one, bonded closer than brothers through combat. To Selk, it was the ultimate drug. Nothing else made him feel anywhere near as good, and not for lack of trying. There was a slight crackle in his ear as the comm activated.

"Eagle squad, check in." It was Colonel Beneton, head of Eagle squad and the ranking officer on this mission. The task force of fifty was split into five squads, each of which was in turn divided into teams Alpha and Bravo, of five soldiers each. He waited for his team leader to speak.

"Eagle Bravo, check in," came the expected voice, right on time. There was something sublimely comforting in military precision, Selk felt. He heard his three other teammates check in, and then did so himself. His team leader then relayed the all-clear to Beneton. The display read thirty seconds.

- - - - -

"So far so good" Hieron muttered to himself as the fleet entered formation around the *Hariasa*. The Hornets had all launched without a hitch, and the Valkyrie had entered a high orbit ready for the deployment stage of the operation. The only thing he did not like about their current situation was the complete lack of opposition. He had not failed to notice that there had been surveillance buoys close to their arrival point, no doubt not only detecting their arrival but predicting by a few seconds thanks to the phenomenon of the hyperspace bow wake. If anyone was monitoring them, they knew the fleet had arrived. So where were they?

"High orbit achieved sir," his navigational officer informed him. "Deployment on schedule for jettison in ten seconds."

"Very good," he replied. "Comm, please monitor our connection to Colonel Beneton throughout the drop and keep me informed if we lose contact at any point."

"Aye sir," came the reply. "Our terminal is pinging his terminal every five seconds."

Hieron could hear the *wham, wham, wham* as each section of escape pods were launched toward the planet. Part of the original plan had seen the *Hariasa* play-acting as if she had been overwhelmed by the expected defenders and evacuated. As defenders of any kind were still notably lacking, they had decided to forego the theatrics.

"This is damned eerie," he stated as he watched the pods silently shrink to specks on the main display screen. "Alright, break orbit and order the fleet into defensive formation. I want Red wing facing one-eighty to watch our six - we don't need any surprises coming up our tail pipe before the ground squads have taken that base out of commission."

The Valkyrie rose from its orbit to take up a position nearby, pointing out into space. The scanners aboard every ship in the fleet were set to maximum, watching and listening for any hint of the threat they all knew was waiting for them somewhere. Tensions were high, and the pilots began to trade insults with one another; though they began as the usual lighthearted banter one always witnessed between nervous soldiers on the edge of a battle, it was not long before true malice was added to the mix and Hieron was forced to override the communication relays.

"Listen up everyone," he said into the comm, the exhaustion of his patience perfectly clear to witness in his voice. "You can bitch and moan as much as you like when we're back, safe and sound, in the hangar. Hell you can settle your differences the old fashioned way if that really takes your fancy. But *right here*, and *right now*, you're on *my* time and under *my* command. Now, I understand you're probably a little nervous because of the lack of enemies to shoot at, and I'm not completely sanguine on that same notion. But very soon we'll have word from our ground forces, and then hopefully we'll have some idea of what's going on here. Until then, shut the fuck up and if you can't get along I'll come out there and shoot you myself." He motioned for the comm officer to reactivate the send function on the fleet's systems. Nobody said a word.

"Sir, I've got Colonel Beneton on the wave," the comm officer reported.

"Alright, put him on."

- - - - -

"That's right sir, we just now made landfall. I would not recommend the experience, but we're all checked in and it seems nobody's the worse for wear. What's more, it seems Larnel Carter knows what he's talking about when it comes to guidance systems - every one of my men have dropped within metres of their destination. The RVs are well underway and we should be ready to advance on our targets in five minutes."

Colonel Beneton took his thumb off the send button on his transmitter and motioned to his second, Eagle Alpha Two. "We're certain this is the RV?" he asked. EA2, a short, boxy man with a shaved head called Wills, nodded.

"All the nav charts show us to be exactly on top of the RV point, sir" Wills rasped in his gravelly voice.

"Good. You remain here and make sure Eagle squad all get here in the next five minutes. I'm going to scout ahead a few hundred. Stay alert."

With that, Colonel Beneton jogged off into the undergrowth, his feet crunching as quietly as he could make them through the six inches of snow. Eagle's objective was what they believed to be the main hangar, distinguished by a great area cleared of trees. There were several large patches of tarmac which the intelligence analysts had identified as portals to the underground hangar. From the size of the clearing it was estimated that no more than four small escort-class fighters would be inside, and it was Eagle squad's objective to put the entire complex out of commission. Two of the other four squads were targeting similar structures, with Sword squad and Wolf squad taking a fuel depot and a residential area respectively. He didn't envy the latter their task, as it was almost certain that it would be difficult to differentiate enemy from non-combatant, and even harder to make the only safe decision. The squad carried stun weapons, of course, but they were not as effective as a rifle at longer ranges.

There were no sounds as he picked his way between the trees, rifle held ready; even the wind seemed to have stopped entirely. Then the branch next to his head exploded in a colourful mix of laser and flame, and he dropped instinctively to the ground, rifle ready but not returning fire. With any luck his would-be assassin would presume him dead. With even greater luck, they might come to investigate. The lack of warning he had had suggested that his assailant was too close for him to risk discovery by alerting Wills and the others; he would have to wait until this problem was dealt with.

He peered carefully about him until he was satisfied that he could see nothing of his attacker with his eyes alone, and lowered his head to look through his rifle's scope. Nothing. He glanced at the tree that had taken the hit for him, and noted carefully from which direction it had been hit; then, with deliberate and agonising slowness, he turned to face that direction, raising his rifle again to scope out his fire sector. Whoever it was, they seemed to be being as careful as he was; no other shots had been fired toward him or indeed in any direction, and try as he might he was unable to detect even the slightest hint of movement. Then he saw it.

At first he thought it was a lump of snow clinging tenaciously to the trunk of a tree just eight metres distant. Then it moved, and his perception of the perspective shifted slightly as he realised that it was the snowsuit-clad elbow of his assailant. Scanning down, he located what he had initially taken to be a rock, half obscured by a thick root, and which he now deduced to be the man's foot. As carefully as he could, Beneton reached one grey-gloved hand down under the snow beneath his chest, his searching fingers settling onto the hard roundness of a stone the size of a grenade. He checked his scope again; still no more movement. Swiftly he threw his arm out, sending the stone soaring through the wood to smack satisfyingly into a tree trunk. His scope was already up to his eye and he saw the rifle swing round from behind the tree, tracking the source of the sound. *Amateur*, Beneton thought as his laser pulse bored through the woman's brain.

"Eagle Alpha Two, Eagle Alpha One," he said quietly into his comm. "Come in Eagle Alpha Two. Over."

"Eagle Alpha One, Eagle Alpha Two," the comm responded in Wills' voice. "I hear you Colonel. Over."

"Hard contact. One female, snowsuit, G-88 concussion rifle. Target has been neutralised. Be advised I am continuing my reconnoitre; follow on my six when the rest of Eagle squad is assembled. Standard wide cover formation. Over."

"Roger that Eagle Alpha One," Wills replied. "Over and out."

Beneton could see the edge of the clearing from where he stood now; there was no sign of any significant structures above ground level, which meant the ventilation and waste management systems were either entirely self-contained or had their inlets and outlets concealed elsewhere. Their first priority was to find a way in; locating these amenities could provide their answer.

There was a low line of shrubs at the edge of the trees, and he dropped to his stomach to crawl through, acquiring more than a few scrapes and cuts from the cruel, thorned branches. Finally he was at the edge of the clearing, and raised his white binoculars to the slit in his white balaclava, hoping anybody who saw him mistook him for a snowdrift. Scanning the area, he could see nothing that might conceal what he sought; there were several places in which the snow was banked higher than in others, but the shapes of these were generally long and squat; not a shape that waste and ventilation outlets tended to take.

A branch rustled behind him, and his hand was on his sidearm in a flash. Wills emerged from behind the tree with the young woman's corpse slowly freezing beside it, glancing at her as he passed. He did not seem to have seen his leader's boots in the thick of the hedge, so Beneton activated his comm.

"Eagle Alpha Two, Eagle Alpha One. Be advised I'm on your twelve o'clock, prone. Over."

"Roger that, Eagle Alpha One," Wills replied, casting his gaze across the line of shrubs until he got a fix on the Colonel's position. Rapidly but stealthily, he made his way to him and suffered the same cuts and grazes on his way through the branches and roots. Beneton waited for him to get settled, then asked for the situation report. "Eagle squad RV'd successfully, sir" Wills reported in a voice barely above a whisper. "I passed on your order to advance, with Alpha team on the left and Bravo on the right. They should all be reaching the clearing about now." Beneton nodded. So far so good. He returned his attention to the clearing, and thought about the next step.

A movement out in the center of the clearing caught his eye. Raising his binoculars, he saw that it was just snow falling down the near side of one of the long drifts. But it was falling too fast, and in too great an amount. Before long, a dark slit opened up in the snow like a seam; he had just enough time to shout a warning to the rest of Eagle squad before the bunker, and three more like it across the clearing, lit up with a withering rain of ruby red laser fire, streaking out at the tree line to the left and right. Hard contact indeed, Beneton thought as he and Wills raised their rifles to return fire.

- - - - -

"Sir, Eagle, Sword, Hawk, and Shield all report hard contact," the comm officer relayed to Hieron, who was pacing impatiently back and forth on the expansive bridge of the *Hariasa*. He stopped in his tracks.

"All of them at once?" he asked.

"So it would seem, sir. Wolf squad are still clear, they are preparing to enter the residential complex." Hieron was getting a distinctly bad feeling about this; it was starting to seem like the enemy were far more organised than previously thought.

"Tell Colonel Peamek to proceed with extreme caution," he instructed, waiting while his order was relayed to the head of Wolf squad, many kilometres below him on the ground. "Anything at all on scanners, ensign?" he asked of the petite young lady stationed at the sensor console.

"Nothing so far, sir" she replied, hands moving confidently across the screen. "Wait, I am detecting a buildup of heat from the surface, consistent with a significant number of ships prepping for launch. It's coming from -" she paused, hands flying back and forth now as she narrowed down the signal. "- all over, sir."

"Come again, ensign?"

"The heat is not confined to any one of the three known launch sites we have targeted with our ground attack," she informed him. "It seems to be spread throughout the whole area between them."

"What could that mean?" he asked, but her reply was drowned out by a shout from the comm officer.

"Sir, Eagle, Hawk and Shield are all reporting in! The launch doors at all three sites are opening up."

"Contact the fleet," Hieron ordered. "Everyone to come about one eighty, including Red Wing - they remain behind us to watch our backs. I want the rest of the fleet pointing at the planet in ten seconds!"

"Aye sir," the comm officer acknowledged, relaying the message. Then he clamped his hand to his ear, scrunching his face into an expression which suggested that he was listening intently to something hard to discern. "Say again, Eagle" he requested. His look of concentration turned to consternation as he heard the message repeated. "Acknowledged Eagle. Out." He spun on his chair to face Hieron. "Sir, Eagle leader reports multiple hostile fighters launching from his position."

"Multiple?" Hieron echoed. "Could he be more specific?"

"Yes sir. He reports twelve launched. Shield and Hawk have reported the same numbers at their locations."

Hieron's heart sank to his stomach. That was three times the estimated capacity of the Korpi base; clearly intel had not bargained on an extensive subterranean complex, with each launch site connected to a central hangar. It was the only thing that would explain what they had seen. He swore, and vowed silently that if he lived through this, he would do something to improve the quality of the intelligence they were receiving.

Before long, the ensign at the sensors console reported the first contact, rising rapidly through the atmosphere followed closely by over thirty others. They were not headed directly for the corporate fleet, but rather at ninety degrees from an intercept course.

"They're looking to form up before taking a run at us," Hieron declared, and ordered the fleet to come about to intercept and engage before the pirates had a chance to form up. The twelve LS-72s, nicknamed Lightnings, streaked off in front of the six slightly slower, more massive Hornets. The *Hariasa* powered along behind, sustaining a respectable pace for such a large ship. The first sparks of exchanged laser fire lit up in the distance. The Battle of Korpi had finally begun.

# Chapter 4

The pirates were caught out of position by the Lightnings as the small, fast ships hit their flank and sparked off an enormous writhing mêlée. The first four explosions came in quick succession as the clumsy or unluckier pilots were thinned from the herd. The pirates were flying a motley assortment of civilian and ex-military fighters, with a few Lightnings and Hornets of their own in the mix. The corporate Lightnings were heavily outnumbered until the Hornets joined the fray, their missiles slicing across the vacuum and striking or missing their targets. Finally, the *Hariasa* pushed its way into the centre of the dogfight, each of its dozen turrets swivelling and firing constantly.

As close as Hieron could tell, the battle was about as close as it could be; the pirates' superior numbers were offset by the corporate fleet's greater firepower and training. The *Hariasa* itself was proving to be a particular asset, as her turrets took a heavy toll on the enemy fighters. Hieron would have liked to take credit for that, but his orders to the crew amounted to little more than 'do what you think is best'. He began to feel more and more out of place without a flight stick in his hand, and caught more than one look of disapproval from Dent. Every few minutes he would request a status update from the fleet; inevitably each time he did, another fighter had been lost.

Direct hits on the *Hariasa* herself were also becoming more frequent, and Hieron was half tempted to sit down in the captain's throne when he was very nearly knocked from his feet for the fifth time. Shields were still holding, though they were becoming seriously drained, and the pirates just kept coming like carrion birds around a dying beast, each taking a nibble and ducking away before they could get bitten themselves. It was not a feeling he relished, to be stuck within that beast and unable to exert the direct control to which he was used. Again he requested an update on the fleet's status.

"Red Wing is gone, sir," the tactical officer informed him. "Green Wing has lost four and five, Blue Wing two, three, and six. Black Wing is still holding but Black Leader is reporting that his shields have been drained. He's trying to hang back and wait for them to recharge, but there aren't too many safe places out there."

"What about the enemy?" Hieron asked.

"Hostile contacts have been reduced to twenty," he was told, "but at this stage of the fight -"

"I know," Hieron interrupted. "Only the best and the luckiest remain." His thoughts were swimming in circles in his head; they were still outnumbered nearly three to one, and their advantage in having troops on the ground had been effectively neutralised by the superior numbers. It had been hoped that they might prevent the launch of the pirate fleet, but their demolition role had now been reduced to an afterthought - everything now rested on the battle in high orbit. He did not care what the corporate heads said - if there was to be another sortie, he would have command of a fighter wing, not a capital ship. He had never felt so powerless.

"Sir, Black Leader is down," the tac officer informed him. "Our shields are at five percent; we can't hold much longer. What are your orders?" That was a good question, Hieron thought. He had no experience of handling a capital ship in combat, and did not know the protocol regarding when it was time to press the attack and when it was time to head on home. Certainly the shields failing was a terrible thing, but this ship had thick skin - how many hits could she take before going down? Finally the decision clicked in his mind, and all doubt was gone.

"Commander Dent, please take command; the bridge is yours." Her surprised expression gave him pause momentarily as it struck him that she was really quite attractive when she was not scowling. He turned to the comm officer. "Tell Black Wing to hold fast; I'll be taking over as Black Leader in about thirty seconds." His command was hesitantly obeyed, and he could see the doubt and disbelief in the officer's eyes. "Don't worry," he addressed the officer and the bridge crew in general. "I'm not abandoning ship, I'm just doing what I should have done as soon as we arrived in the system. I am not cut out for command of capital ships." He made for the door, and paused briefly. "Good luck, everyone. I will be commanding the fleet from my Hornet, but if I'm lost, Commander Dent is in charge."

He ran down the corridors, taking a left, then a right, and then several more until he was half running, half falling through the doorway of the cargo bay, thirstily drinking in the view of his TA-69 Hornet. He leapt up the ladder two rungs at a time, and grabbed his helmet from the seat, his body following the old routine of preflight without his conscious input. Activating the comm, he addressed the fleet.

"This is Black Leader. Stay clear of the port-side cargo doors, I'm on my way out. Black Two and Black Three, prepare to form up on my four and eight. The rest of Black Wing provide as much cover as you can manage." Several acknowledgments echoed into his head, and he smiled. He was back where he belonged. The canopy closed, the engines roared, the cargo bay doors opened, and he was out in the thick of the biggest dogfight he had ever witnessed.

Within a few seconds he was clear, and noted with satisfaction that two Hornets had formed up on his wings, anticipating his turns as well as any wingmen of his ever had. He immediately throttled up and threw his Hornet at a pirate Tercel who was dogging a Lightning from Green Wing. The corporate fighter was putting her pursuer through some tight turns in an effort to shake him, and the Tercel was itself difficult to follow as a result. Hieron still managed to get a few shots on target, but it was clear that the Lightning would be toast by the time he finished off the Tercel.

"Black One, high hard right, Black Two, low hard left" he ordered. "Let's pin this bastard down."

The formation of Hornets widened across a diagonal axis, and the widening of their fire sector resulted in more hits landing on target, draining the pirate's shields. Soon he was nothing more than a cloud of debris, and the Lightning was free to pursue her own targets.

"Black Leader, Green Leader" she said. "Thanks for the assist."

"You're welcome, Green Leader" he replied. "Repay me sometime."

The fighting was intense, and more than once the small formation of

Hornets gained pursuers of their own, but for the most part these were easily dealt with by a transient breaking of formation, the two wingmen veering off and around behind the pirates to ruin their day permanently. Hieron allowed his hopes to raise slightly when he took the next head count. Green Wing had lost another, but the enemy were down to fifteen. With their superior ships, the advantage now lay with the corporate fleet. If they were careful, and lucky, it was all but over. The ground battle remained, of course, but with their remaining fighters they would be able to pull off a significant air strike to soften the target for the ground troops.

Years later, when he recalled the events of the next few minutes, Hieron would find it difficult to convince himself that he had not been dreaming. That his flight recorder would confirm the evidence of his own eyes merely made him doubt the reliability of the technology. Nevertheless, carved indelibly upon his memory forevermore were the words of the young ensign manning the sensors aboard the *Hariasa*.

"Black Leader be advised, fresh contact bearing two seven eight from our current course. Four hundred clicks and closing fast."

"Identify," he ordered.

"Unknown as yet, sir," she replied, as another pirate met his explosive end in Hieron's crosshairs. "Based on their current speed and course they will be on us within one minute." That couldn't be right; nothing travelled that fast in sub-light.

"Check that, ensign," he told her. "Confirm one minute?"

"Confirmed sir," her voice sounded as perplexed as he was. "The contact is approaching at a speed of approximately eight kilometres per second." There was a pause, but the comm had not disconnected. "Something else, sir" she added eventually. "We are reading a massive heat buildup on the surface of the planet below our position."

Hieron groaned to himself; more pirates is the one thing he could definitely do without. They had a chance against the fighters that still remained in the space above Korpi, but as few as two more could tip the balance fatally. A retreat at this stage would be an horrifically messy operation, he knew; not only would they have to attempt to break contact with the remaining fighters and make a clean run to safe jump distance, but he would have no choice but to abandon their ground forces in hostile territory. Fifty men and women who would not be coming home with the fleet, perhaps never. The comm officer spoke next.

"Sir, we have Colonel Beneton of Eagle squad on the box."

"Patch him through to me," Hieron ordered as he dodged a poorly-aimed missile and reciprocated with one of his own, which struck and destroyed its target. "Talk to me Beneton. How many have launched this time?"

"Uh, none sir," came the gruff but uncertain response against a background of laser fire. "That's what I was telling your comm officer. We're still pinned down at the launch site, but there are no ships launching to correspond to your heat buildup. But that's not the strangest thing," he added. "The snow is melting."

"Eagle leader, say again. The snow is melting?" Hieron was starting to think he was losing his mind, but so far it seemed he was in good company if that were the case.

"The snow is melting, sir," Beneton confirmed. "It just started a minute ago. It was in drifts all around, but now there's hardly a chunk left bigger than my fist. My gauges are reading temp at fifteen Celsius and rising; it's going to get uncomfortable in these suits soon," he supplied as an afterthought.

"All right Colonel," Hieron responded, trying to sound more confident than he felt. "Hold position and await further intel. Tomac out."

He checked his scanner; if the estimate was correct, the new contacts should be in range of his more limited sensors very soon. Just as he glanced down, he saw it: a shape that rivalled moons for size, advancing at a velocity of which no known vessel was capable. Something that big should be visible to the naked eye, he thought, and looked up. There was nothing there, where he should have seen an enormous shape eclipsing the Xylon sun. Something may have gleamed briefly, but it could just as easily have been his imagination playing tricks on him. He decided to contact the *Hariasa* for a second pair of eyes.

"*Hariasa* this is Black Leader. Do we have eyes on the new contact?"

"Affirmative, sir" came the response, the words more confident than the voice. "It's not a fleet, at least not in the way we would understand the word. It seems to be a huge structure of wires, like a net in the shape of a globe." That would explain why he could see nothing from his cockpit, Hieron thought, but not why an object that was composed primarily of nothing would show up as such a large contact on his scanner. Unless the grid were energised somehow.

- - - - -

He could see the bunkers clearly now, a series of dark slits looking out menacingly from low concrete structures, barely half a metre visible above the ground. He was also painfully aware that he, all of his men, and the other squads, were all quite conspicuously visible in their white snowsuits, contrasted now as they were against the dark greens and browns of the forest. He swore. Things were truly not looking positive for the ground troops; he hoped that they were at least going well for the fleet, high above him - then they might get some air support.

He desperately needed it, he admitted to himself; those bunkers were obstinately refusing to crack, despite the ordnance he had thrown at them - both precision sniping from the sharpshooters and artillery from the heavy weapons specialists. The concrete structures showed signs of these efforts, a number of black scars marring their otherwise monotonous grey surfaces, but were otherwise unaffected. The frontal assault option was well and truly exhausted.

He therefore took it as a sign from God when Eagle Bravo reported in that they had located one of their objectives - an air vent outlet, carefully disguised as a tree approximately a kilometre from the centre of the clearing. It was not even close to being wide enough for a man to fit through, but with a bit of help from heavy explosives, it could be widened. He ordered this to be done, with the charges placed strategically so as to avoid as much rubble as possible falling back into the hole created.

Beneton kept his head down as much as possible while he backed out through the hedge, feeling the fresh cuts it was providing for his trouble. The occasional pot-shot still whipped over his head, smacking into the trees or streaking off into the distance behind him. He thought he felt the ground shake a little as Eagle Bravo reported the vent breached, and he rose to a stoop to make his way quickly and quietly through the sodden undergrowth, boots sinking into the moist ground as he did so.

By the time he reached the breach, he had gathered the rest of Alpha team to him - with the exception of Wills, who had caught an unlucky shot square in the forehead just an hour ago. The hole was a mess of dirt, concrete, and bent girders, but at its centre was something that warmed the Colonel's heart: a gap, big enough for a man to fit through, with artificial light shining through it like some strange subterranean heaven. He looked around at Eagle squad, noting in their eyes the same frustration and eagerness as he himself was feeling.

"Good work, Bravo," he told them, aware of the command advantages of positive reinforcement. "Get some flashbangs down there and we go in - all of us. Alpha first, to set up defensive positions, then Bravo. Our objectives haven't changed since the briefing, gentlemen - this base still needs to be neutralised. Once we have this launch site reduced to rubble, we contact the other squads and see if they're in need of assistance. When and only when this rock is swept clean do we get to go home." He cocked his rifle and smiled a grim smile. "What are we waiting for?"

There was enough concrete and twisted steel fallen into the corridor below that Alpha were able to set up strong defensive positions against the hail of fire that met them once the dust had cleared and the effects of the flashbangs had worn off. Without their advantage of the bunkers, the pirates in the facility showed their lack of expertise against the well-trained and more disciplined mercenary troops. The dozen or so that had made their way to the site of the blast were dealt with by vengeful and ruthless efficiency by the soldiers who only a brief time ago had been at their mercy.

The laser fire stopped, and Beneton ordered his squad forward to the corner of the corridor ahead to secure the area. The other direction was blocked by a security door which had buckled, either from the blast or the steel support which had collapsed into it. He called up for Bravo to join them, and soldiers began to fall into the corridor like heavily armed, purposeful raindrops. The word came from ahead that the way was clear, and they advanced as a single unit, with two men watching the rear, stepping carefully backwards as they entrusted their lives to the others as surely as the men facing forward entrusted theirs to those in the rear.

Half the opposition they met turned and ran at the mere sight of the seven mercenaries, all semblance of discipline deserting them as they came face to face with those who murder for a living rather than only when it was necessary. Those who stood their ground did not do so for long, and the careful backward pacing of the rearguard would occasionally have to make way for a corpse.

The first room they reached the purpose of which was clear was the barracks, given away by the lines of bunk beds and the locker room through which they entered. They swept it clean, though there were few enough pirates inside, and Beneton gathered them in the locker room.

"So far so good, then," he began. "Now, we have no idea of the layout of this facility, so we're either going to have to work it out as we go along, or find some charts someplace. At the very least, we know that the main launch pads are approximately half a click in that direction" he indicated the way they were headed. "Sooner or later we'll come to a fork in the way, and we'll split. Radio contact is to be maintained at all times, unless ordered otherwise." He wiped a gloved hand across his forehead. "Also, it's getting damned hot in here. Let's get these snowsuits off." They all removed the lightweight, insulated white coveralls, the snowy balaclavas, and the thick gloves. What remained was a simple black uniform with their mercenary insignia at the shoulder. Beneton felt much better to have taken off the stifling outer layers, and he could see the same relief mirrored in the faces of his soldiers.

They moved swiftly and efficiently through the corridors and rooms of the facility, clearing each area and moving on, killing without a second thought all opposition. As Beneton had predicted, the way forked before long, so Alpha and Bravo teams went their separate ways, maintaining radio contact as instructed, and reporting every enemy contact and successful kill in their accustomed military brevity. As they made their way as best they could toward the primary hangar, the increase in heat was noticeable. Perhaps, Beneton thought, there was a fire inside; it was not uncommon for all the fuel, an inevitable part of launch sites, to spark a conflagration. That hypothesis was lent more weight as they finally came upon the hangar blast doors, ten metres square and probably as thick as a man's head was wide. They were definitely warm to the touch.

Bravo One's voice rattled into the corridor, reporting that they had reached the door on the other side of the hangar. Beneton had one of his team check the controls, and as they seemed to be operational, he ordered a synchronised double breach - opening the doors on each side of the hangar at once, Alpha and Bravo would enter in a standard cover procedure they had practised endlessly, hoping to thereby take whatever occupants there might be all at once and by surprise. He warned both teams to expect extreme conditions on the inside - if there was indeed a fire, there would be no telling how widespread it was until they were through the doors.

They executed the manoeuvre and were surprised to find not only that there was no fire, but no sign of opposition either. The hangar was completely empty, with the exception of a few dozen packing crates and fuel drums. The place was immense, easily ten times the size they had been expecting each of the individual landing pads to be; the large doors in the roof that had led to this mistaken belief were hanging wide open, letting the bright daylight fall in from the surface. The sun was high in the sky and the mercenaries were sweating within seconds from the increased heat.

Having secured the whole length and breadth of the enormous room, with every corner and catwalk cleared, they gathered in the centre to discuss their next move.

"Well it may be too early to say it" Beneton began, unsuccessfully wiping the sweat from his head with an equally sweat-soaked palm, "but it looks like we got them all. Next order of business is to confirm that by securing the entire facility, front to back. I would estimate we've only seen half of the corridors in this place so far. Then we'll work out where to use our explosives to best effect to wipe this place out." He dabbed at his face with his sleeve. "Secondary objective is to find the air conditioning," he half-joked as each team picked up their gear and moved out, back through the doors by which they had entered.

- - - - -

Hieron was unsure which had been more incredible - that the strange net sphere had stopped so abruptly after having travelled at speeds faster than any known vessel, or that when it did so, it had opened. It now appeared as a flat, flower shaped net hanging in space parallel to the planet, completely motionless. The energy readings they had detected were definitely originating from the object, and the sensor operative aboard the *Hariasa* professed to be fairly confident that the energy was being directed at the surface of Korpi. Hieron hoped that it wasn't the cause of the increased temperatures that Beneton and the other squads had reported, but he suspected that that hope would turn out to be a vain one.

But what purpose could this object have in warming up the surface? Was it something the pirates had discovered and were now using to thwart the invasion, perhaps? The ground teams were, after all, reporting that all hostiles had disappeared quite suddenly; that would certainly be consistent with the deployment of a weapon of mass destruction. Of course, that still left open the question of where the object had come from in the first place - but that question was glaring at them whichever hypothesis they chose.

The battle in orbit was starting to wane, with only two hostile fighters remaining. Finally, they apparently decided it was not worth staying any longer, and they turned to run. It was, Hieron mused, probably not the wisest decision when you were surrounded by pilots who you had just spent the better part of an hour trying to kill, and who had lost friends in the battle, flying vessels every bit as fast as your own. They were dust within seconds, and all that remained of the corporate fleet were two Hornets, one Lightning, and the *Hariasa*, with her pockmarked hull and conspicuous place where a wing used to be. In terms of personnel, the fleet itself had sustained perhaps fifty percent losses - not counting the ground troops.

Hieron was pulling back into formation with the *Hariasa* with the two other remaining fighters when the comm officer contacted him again. "Sir, urgent message from Colonel Senda, patching through." Colonel Senda was the somewhat haughty leader of Shield squad, who had apparently turned to military service after an unsuccessful twenty years in middle management. That rumour was lent more weight every time Hieron spoke to the man; he was the most utterly frustrating person he had ever met. But none of that was evident in the exchange that followed; the usually arrogant and unfazed Senda sounded genuinely worried.

"Mr Tomac, this is Colonel Senda of Shield squad. Two of my team have collapsed from the heat down here; we're staying in the shade as much as we can, but if we don't think of something soon we're going to sweat to death." That was enough for Hieron to confirm that his suspicions - or rather those of the sensor operative - had been correct. The object was the cause of the rising temperature, and if it continued to raise it, the entirety of the mercenary ground force would die from the heat. He told Senda to stand by and opened a channel to the *Hariasa*.

"Commander Dent, this is Black Leader," he began. "That object is almost certainly going to kill everything and everyone on the surface. Can you get down there to pick them up?"

"I seriously doubt it," she replied. "Even if we made it to the surface in one piece, the ascent would finish us off for sure. We're in truly bad shape over here - limping home is about all we can hope for."

"Acknowledged. Any success with trying to communicate with that thing?" he asked.

"Negative," came the reply. "All attempts have been met with stony silence. If anyone's in the array, they're not talking."

"The array?" he repeated. "That's what we're calling it?"

"It was ensign Sutter's choice of word," she responded. "It seemed to fit, so that's how we've been referring to it over here. Unless you have any objections?"

"Not at all, I've been thinking of it as 'object' and 'thing'. I'd say 'array' is an improvement." He quickly contacted the squad leaders on the surface and told them the situation with the array, and that they might be best served getting as far away from the pirate base as they could in the next ten minutes. He cut off their protests and resumed the connection to Dent. "One way or another we need to make it stop. If we go back for reinforcements, the mercs will be dead before it arrives. Launch a missile - just a warning shot, detonate it a hundred metres to the starboard side of the array."

"If it's nothing more than a weapon, that won't do anything," Dent objected. "We need to get over there an dismantle it, forcefully if necessary."

"I'd love to," he retorted, "but my fleet is a little shaken up at the moment. If there's a chance we can scare this thing off, I'd like to take that chance. Launch the missile." She said nothing else, but he watched as the missile shot out toward the array, hoping it would have the effect he wanted, but knowing that Dent was probably right; nothing was going to happen.

They were both wrong. As the missile erupted on target, one hundred metres away from the array, dozens of tiny objects broke away from the centre of the 'flower' and shot towards them. Not wanting to take any chances, Hieron ordered evasive manoeuvres and kicked his Hornet into a wild, high ascent to port. The *Hariasa* was less able to respond with any speed, but launched a cloud of countermeasures to her fore before turning to bolt as fast as she could. His scanner was unable to identify the objects as either missiles or spaceships, and somewhere subconsciously Hieron finally admitted to himself the possibility that they were dealing with truly alien technology.

The first of the objects intercepted the *Hariasa*'s countermeasures and stopped before it. Hieron was unable to see, either with his eyes or the scanner, what happened next; a second later the countermeasure was gone. The object, joined by many of the others, continued on to the next countermeasure, and then the next. Before long there were none left, and they moved on to track the fighters and the Valkyrie, unerringly following the path they had taken with their evasive flying. Hieron saw them gather around the Lightning, and watched as they cut it easily into small chunks, trying not to notice that some of those chunks were leaking red fluid.

"That does it," he said. "Dent, Black Three, get the hell out of here - we're no match for this thing yet. We'll come back with reinforcements as soon as we can."

"Damn it Tomac," Dent shouted back. "There are fifty men and women on the surface of that planet! We can't just abandon them to die!"

"We both know they're already dead," he replied as he watched the things converge with the *Hariasa*. "It must be a hundred Celsius down there by now. We try to rescue them, we're all dead. Now get your ass into hyperspace!" There was a hard silence before she responded.

"Yes, *sir*." She did not need to specify that the order was being obeyed under strenuous protest; her tone did that more than adequately in her stead. The *Hariasa* was already at a safe jump distance from the gravity well of the planet, and she began powering her hyperdrive, drifting without forward acceleration as she did so. It was a shortcoming of the dual engine design that the sub-light drive had to be shut down before the hyperspace field generator would come online. He flicked the switch for his own and watched as the objects closed with him, entirely helpless until the field was generated. Fortunately, being in a smaller craft, he did not have to wait as long as those in the *Hariasa* for the field to reach a suitable strength. It was up to one hundred percent in just a few seconds, and as his ship began its familiar trembling, he looked to port and saw the *Hariasa*, not seventy metres away, being swarmed by the small objects from the array.

From this distance, he could see what was happening as tiny, continuous laser beams were emitted by the objects, cutting ruthlessly through the Valkyrie's shields and hull. His heart was in his throat as she began to come apart, the lethal nothing that surrounded her rushing in to destroy all signs of life within. He froze, dread sinking heavily into every part of his body as one of the things appeared outside his window, looking distinctly alien and yet somehow resembling a fish of some kind. It was brown, about half the size of a Lightning, and had a circular opening that looked disturbingly like a mouth on the front. Further details escaped him as he disappeared from the Xylon system altogether, the strange emptiness of hyperspace descending around the canopy.

Beneath his former position high above the planet Korpi, forty corpses lay quietly cooking among the burning trees. Though he never saw them, that image would haunt him for the rest of his life.

# Part 2
## Chapter 5

Nobody brought up Max's previous departure from the group two weeks ago, nor that he had treated them to an abridged version the following week. It was impossible to tell whether this silence had its roots in a desire to get along, a general fear of confrontation, or social awkwardness; certainly the entirety of the Progressive Policy Debate Forum - barring their insouciant founder - qualified for all three possibilities. Whatever the case, Max now sat in his accustomed chair, with a milky and heavily-sugared coffee on the table in front of him. He stroked his beard, looking around at them as they digested what he had just told them.

"If I had skipped watching the news last night, I never would have believed it," Neri said, finally. Cerydwyn nodded, Max smiled, and Thom was entirely impassive.

"Perhaps now you will accept what I've been telling you all for years. The corporations have admitted they are attempting to form a hegemonic council, pooling their military assets and using that combined power to crush the independent people of the outlier systems."

"I think we're a little way off you being right about everything, Max," Thom responded derisively. "The facts of the matter as they stand are that A: seven corporations have been cooperating recently, putting aside their customary rivalries to mount a campaign against those in the outlier systems who have, for some time, been harassing their trade routes. B: the recent sortie, apparently targeting the Xylon system, resulted in a victory - albeit a pyrrhic one. C: the corporations

55

are now appealing for more of their smaller counterparts to join them in the rest of the campaign so that their victories are a little more decisive from now on." Max began to object, but Thom held up a commanding finger of silence. "There is no evidence, none *at all*, either to suggest that this defeat is being blamed on aliens, or that the allied corporations are planning to take command of anything more than their amalgamated fleet."

"The evidence you seek is right under your nose!" Max shouted, his eyes wide and brow furrowed with anger. "If only you will stop blindly trusting the media to tell you what's really going on - even they are mindlessly recycling what the corporations are telling them. I know we are meant to be a society of idealists, but there's a world of difference between wanting the best of all possible worlds and believing that you already live there." He sighed and relaxed back into his seat, his short rant out of fuel. "I don't know why they haven't blamed their recent heavy losses on aliens," he continued after a brief pause. "It's the strategy that makes the most sense politically."

"But didn't you say that you had a source who told you for sure what they were planning?" Neri asked, carefully trying to phrase the question in such a way as to avoid another outburst. Max had the good grace to look sheepish when he finally answered her a few moments later, after staring long and hard at his cooling coffee.

"To be honest, I filled that detail in myself," he admitted. "My source only told me they were planning to use the campaign against the so-called 'pirates' to attempt to unite the central planets under a single government, then expand outwards. The alien assault gambit is just how I thought they would go about it - use a huge, unknown and terrifying threat to spark off panic throughout the inhabited worlds, appeal for unity, and seize the power that the masses will only too gladly surrender to you. An anti-pirate campaign would provoke mixed and equivocal support at best; nobody in the core considers them a serious threat to their own way of life. It makes no sense," he added, returning to stare at the nearly-white coffee, watching it warm the table.

"Maybe they'll choose that tactic if the pirate thing doesn't work like they hope" supplied Cerydwyn, trying to make Max feel better; she had always been the most tolerant toward his strange habits, and the others often suspected she had feelings for him. He just smiled a weak smile at her and remained silent.

- - - - -

Kiah was, all things considered, in quite a good mood. Granted, the assault on Korpi had been a barely-mitigated disaster, the apparent destruction of the pirate base eclipsed wholly by the massacre of over one hundred and forty men and women. But every cloud had a silver lining, as they said, and his task had just been made much easier - almost too easy, if it weren't for the problem of Hieron. The man had returned, offered his report in a concise and professional manner, and promptly disappeared into his quarters. Anyone who had tried to talk to him had been met with silence over the intercom, and after three days they had forced the door to check he was still alive. They found him sat on his bunk, unshaven and unwashed, staring at the wall. Alive, certainly, but only by a somewhat narrow definition of the word.

So it was that Kiah Sicarius, the Primus' representative to the corporate allies, was required to marshal all of his spiritual education and set forth to break Hieron out of the prison he had made for himself - or at least to get him to eat something; that was what General Leetman had described as a 'primary objective'. Snapping him out of it she had described as secondary. Kiah was not sure he shared her view of the priorities, given the importance of Hieron to the Church's agenda.

Finally he reached Hieron's door, and keyed the intercom - not that he expected a response, but he was a keen proponent of courtesy in every situation. He was not surprised to find that he had to enter the override code on the keypad to gain entry, stepping into the darkness beyond. After the bright whiteness of the corridor, it took a few moments for his eyes to adjust to the gloom, which he later counted as a blessing as it prevented him being struck by the full horror of Hieron's appearance all at once. Never before had Kiah seen a man so utterly bereft of joy, and the sight of it cut him deeply. He had always had a great capacity for empathy, and had never until now considered it a handicap in any way.

He knelt in front of the broken pilot, tears in his eyes as he contemplated the thoughts that he imagined floating menacingly in the man's head. It was as if he could see into Hieron's mind, haunted by what he had seen in orbit of Korpi, and what he had been forced to do, in abandoning the mercenaries on the surface. It was not his fault, of course, but that was virtually irrelevant when the grief was this deep. It would not erase the charred faces, the floating chunks of asphyxiated corpse, or the imagined screams of the dying from his mind. There were no words that would suffice, so Kiah lifted his hand to place it gently, and he hoped comfortingly, on Hieron's shoulder. He stayed like that for what seemed like hours, staring into those empty eyes, until finally his gaze was met.

Fresh tears welled anew in Kiah's eyes as he saw the purest pain behind the dark irises. He truly believed that the eyes were the window to the soul, and what he saw as he gazed in through Hieron's was the torment of the survivor, the guilt of being the only one left after a massacre. That he had been in command of every man and woman killed only compounded his grief. In that moment, Kiah knew exactly what this pilot, raised so far to fall so soon, was thinking: he wanted to die. That Kiah knew, just as surely as he knew that it was his duty to prevent him in any way he could. Taking eye contact as a sign that communication might be possible at last, he spoke.

"Hieron, I cannot imagine what you must be feeling," he lied, knowing exactly. "I am here as a friend, and as a representative of the Church, to save you from yourself." He paused, trying to gauge a reaction in the pilot's blank face. "What do you know of our Church and its mission?"

"Unity," Hieron muttered, his voice cracking with disuse. A first step toward victory - communication had been restored.

"That's right, the unity of faith, and of humanity through that faith. You know of course of our efforts in the twenty-first century to bring all the Earth's faiths together under one banner - no dogma but what we already shared in common, one shared faith joined together to unite the world instead of divide it. It was a beautiful vision, and it truly took a hold when we demonstrated its power in the Middle East. From that day, we have gone from strength to strength, offering something for everyone no matter in which direction your spiritualism lies. I have never asked you this before, because I believe everyone has a right to privacy in spiritual matters, but are you a member of the Church of Intentionality?" Hieron shook his head slightly.

"Well I don't intend to pressure you one way or another, but know that the Church is here to provide whatever support you need. Many find it comforting to believe that their lives are but a part of a vast cosmic plan, playing out like clockwork in every corner of the universe. We do not pretend to know the intelligence that lies behind the plan, but merely acknowledge its existence. God is as good a word as any."

No reaction. "What I'm saying, Hieron, is that there was no way for you to prevent what happened; it was not your fault, it was an inevitable part of the universal plan. I mourn those we lost as much as anyone, but more than that I celebrate their contribution to the Great Destiny; they gave all that they had to the universe, and God is grateful."

No more words came from the pilot before him, so he decided that he had said enough for one day. He rose, stooping again to plant a kiss on Hieron's forehead, lingering slightly as he did so. "Blessings upon you, Hieron Tomac," he said, and left the room.

- - - - -

The primary topic of discussion around the conference table was what to do next. As ever, the opinion was split between the seven corporate heads and the lone General - some wanted to retaliate immediately with everything they had at their disposal, others wanted to retreat completely and make their stand, eventually and if necessary, on Earth itself. Opinion was even split on whether Hieron's report had been accurate in its interpretations - how did they know that the technology he had witnessed was alien in origin? Those who voiced the latter opinion were the ones who had argued against releasing that detail to the media at this early stage.

"The flight recorder has all the information we need," Parnett rumbled, speaking up out of frustration after an hour of his customary silence. "Clearly the design of the array is like nothing we have ever designed or seen - and the speeds it reached are simply unheard of in cosmonautics. There was no hyperspace bow wake detected, so it is reasonable to hypothesise that they have no such capability. As ridiculous as it sounds, the most rational conclusion to reach from the evidence before us is that this array was our first contact with an alien civilisation. It is dangerous to assume otherwise," he added.

"What we need," Balfour asserted, "is a reconnaissance sortie to assess the situation. Check they're still there, maybe probe their defences."

Dang Zhou scoffed loudly. "What we need," he retorted hotly, "is to gather up every last scrap of military hardware we control and throw it as hard as we can against this thing. Just because it caught us with our pants down this time doesn't mean it's a match for us when we're well prepared."

"No," Venk disagreed nasally. "We must fall back and regroup, concentrate our defence across a smaller perimeter. I'm not saying we go all the way back to Earth," she assured them when they groaned as one. "I'm just saying that we're spread too thinly - who's to say where they will strike next?"

"Have we all forgotten about diplomacy?" Ari Zack asked quietly. "What we need to do is try talking to the array; our first attempt failed, certainly, but we have other methods we can try."

"What we need is consensus," a voice said from the door, and they did not need to turn and look to know that it was Kiah who stood there, white hair illuminated further by the gleaming corridor beyond. "We will achieve nothing decisive if all we do is sit here and bicker, eventually settling on a course of action that is such a compromise that it lacks the power to truly achieve anything."

"Let me guess," Gendson growled, not bothering to hide his distaste for the white-haired man, "you're the one to give us this consensus, whether we agree with it or not."

"Not I, my friends" Kiah replied. "Hieron Tomac is the man to unite us." Silence fell across the conference table, a strange and uncomfortable silence. It was Larnel Carter, of all people, who finally broke it.

"Hieron Tomac is a vegetable, Sicarius. Worse than that, he's a vegetable that failed to prevent a massacre and may have doomed us all by assaulting that array. Nobody will want to follow him."

"My dear Carter," Kiah smiled. "They *will* follow him, and so will you. It is inevitable."

- - - - -

Klaira Destri wandered quiet and alone through the corridors of the station, her thoughts confused and conflicted. *So many dead*, she kept thinking, *so many friends*. Part of her wanted to hate Tomac - for abandoning them, for surviving - she wasn't sure which. But a stronger part remembered meeting the man, remembered his kindness and humour, and knew that this had probably hit him hardest of all. She could well imagine the places his mind was taking him now, and she knew only too well where those paths could lead. Something deep within her refused to allow that to happen, and before she was conscious of her whereabouts, she was standing outside his quarters, fingers hovering over the intercom. She did not know what she was going to do if he answered, but she pressed the button anyway.

No response. She tried again, and leaned in close to the microphone. "M-Mr Tomac?" she asked, quietly and hesitantly. "It's me. I mean, Technician Destri. Klaira. We met shortly before the ... during the week of training. May I come in?" It was not the most gracious of requests, but it was clearly good enough, because the door slid aside to reveal a haggard, sleep-deprived man with dark circles around his eyes and several days of hair growth on his face. But what stood out most was the utter despair in his gaze; it stirred memories Klaira had fought long and hard to push to the back of her mind. Her father, a mining foreman on Hephaestus, returning home one day with that selfsame look in his eyes; and the horrors of what had followed. She shook herself mentally, forcing herself back into the present.

Hieron hardly gave her more than a glance before returning to his apparently accustomed place sat on the edge of the low metal bunk. The sheets were slightly crumpled but nevertheless appeared not to have been slept in. A couple of ration packets lay strewn on the floor; at least he was eating. She crossed the few paces to the bed and sat down next to him, unsure of what she should be saying or doing.

"Had many visitors?" she asked finally, opting for small talk over nothing.

"Kiah," he murmured in response.

"The white-haired man from the Church?" she asked. She had seen him around Alamo Station once or twice, and against her better judgement could not help but find him a little unsettling. Hieron simply grunted in confirmation.

"Did he help at all?" she inquired. "I know the Church can be a great comfort in times of stress." Hieron shrugged.

"Told me it was destiny," he mumbled, his tone conveying exactly how convinced he had been by that argument.

"Perhaps he is right," Klaira told him. "The Church is very wise in these

61

matters." Another shrug. She decided to change her approach.

"From what I hear, you know, in the canteen and everything," she told him quietly, leaning in as if to take him into her confidence, "things are a real mess up at the top. All the corporate heads are just sat around arguing; nothing's getting done, even now, when the ar- ... when danger could be approaching" she finished. "They need you." She looked up at him, drawing his eyes to her own. "We all need you." He made a sound that was halfway between a scoff and a sob, turning away from her as he did so. She gathered her courage, and steeled her nerves.

"When I was sixteen, I was an apprentice technician at Godsforge. My father had gotten me the job through him being foreman of one of their main supply mines. One day there was an accident, and seventy six people were killed in a cave-in when a pocket of gas was accidentally ignited. My father was the only person to make it out of the shaft alive. When he came home that night he - he barely spoke a word. The next morning I took him his breakfast and found him still sleeping. It was only when I saw the empty bottles of pain pills and whiskey on the floor that I realised he wasn't sleeping." The tears were flowing freely down her face and her chest felt heavy, but she was determined not to start sobbing; she wasn't looking for his pity and comfort, at least not today. She tentatively put a small, comforting hand on his own.

"My mother had left my sister and I when we were both very young. With my father gone, I was supporting us both on an apprentice's wages. There were times we barely scraped by." She sighed a deep and faltering sigh. "What I'm telling you is that however much it hurts, it will not be improved by landing everyone else in the shit." She hadn't meant for her words to become so harsh, but there was no stopping it now. "There are people who rely on you - we could be hours away from another massacre and all those stuffed shirts can do is argue! But at least *they're* doing something - at least they're not just sat in their room staring at the wall waiting for the galaxy to stop spinning." She stood up and faced him.

"Did you hear me?" She demanded, her voice raised. "I said we could be hours away from another massacre. Even if the last one wasn't your fault, which is probably true, if you sit here and do nothing while those seven arrogant bastards *fail* to come to some kind of agreement, then this one *will* be your fault!" Hieron said nothing, and remained where he was, staring blankly at the wall. Klaira shook her head in disgust, and walked out of his room without saying another word.

Two hours later, the door to the conference room opened and Hieron stepped through, clean clothes on his freshly-washed back, shaved chin held defiantly high. He offered himself as an advisor, and they made a space for him at the table without a word of complaint. It would not be long before the standard venom was back in full flow across the room, but for a moment, respect held sway in the silence.

# Chapter Six

The representatives from Earth arrived the next day amid much excitement in the station's primary hangar; many of the men and women working for the corporations had never even met someone from their ancestral home before, much less visited the planet itself. So even if they had been nothing but farmhands, the passengers aboard the shuttle that docked that morning would have been instant celebrities on the station.  As it happened, they were quite used to the attention, being some of the uppermost dignitaries of the Earth States Commonwealth.  Though the vast majority of the galaxy's planets, moons, and space stations were owned and run by the various corporations, the Earth States Commonwealth retained its power over them by having set itself up as the arbitration forum for trade disputes.  Furthermore, any corporation that wished to stake a claim to territory out in the wider galaxy was required to have their headquarters located on Terran soil.

They wasted no time in getting down to business, and after a complete briefing regarding the events in the Xylon system, they joined the discussions of what was to be done next.  Four of the six, it seemed, were fully in favour of joining their own military assets with those of the corporations, the better to defend against this new and major threat.  The remaining two were reluctant, based mainly on distrust of the corporate heads; if Earth's considerable military strength was to be marshalled under one banner, they were adamant that it be the banner of Earth, not the combined banner of the corporate militias.  This became the primary point of debate around the table, and the subject of many heated exchanges and raised voices.

Hieron remained silent throughout, listening to each person speak - or shout - their piece. Eventually, the conversation shifted to the matter of keeping the public informed; again, opinion was split, but this time there appeared to be more voices in favour of telling the people the truth about Xylon than against. The African representative, for one, was adamant that information must be made freely available; the European delegate, however, had a more cautious argument.

"We must not expose ourselves" he asserted, the merest hint of an Italian accent colouring his words. "If we go public with a story about an alien attack, then either we get what we want - full public support - or we don't. The latter could include us not being believed at all, or public sympathy for the aliens themselves, or perhaps just plain panic. We don't want rioting and looting on the streets of Earth; we want calm confidence in our leadership. I am not so sure that full freedom of information is the way to achieve that goal."

"Nobody is going to be calmly confident in the leadership of a group as disparate as ourselves," Kiah declared. "The enmity of these seven corporations alone is all too well known, and there is not a chance that this group could inspire anything grander than cautious optimism." He held up a hand at their complaints and protests. "I am sorry to put it so bluntly, but the time has come for plain speaking. I suggest that our needs - and those of humanity as a whole - will be best served by appointing a spokesperson, one figure through whom we communicate with the public at large. It will convey a sense of unity which is more important than ever at times of dire need." He paused, and indicated Hieron, sat to his left. "I suggest Mr Tomac for this role. If nothing else, he is the only one among us to have witnessed the power of this array, and can therefore be relied upon to communicate this clearly and unequivocally." The North American representative, a Mexican with a long black ponytail, began to object.

"But he's -" he hesitated, looking apprehensively at the pilot across the table. Whatever he was about to say, he decided against it and fell silent. Kiah leaned in toward Hieron.

"Perhaps, my friend, it would be better if you sat this out. Some of these people might not be so polite as our American friend here, and I don't see a slew of insults doing your nerves any good. We'll discuss the matter and call you back when we're finished." He flashed a friendly smile and Hieron departed without a word. Kiah turned to face the Mexican.  "You were about to say something?" he asked.

"Hieron Tomac is a disaster area," the man finished quietly, in case Hieron was still within earshot.

"Which makes him the perfect candidate," Carter noted, the revelation lighting his face.  "Yes, I see now - he's the only choice.  We allow him to address the entire galaxy in a short message telling them of the danger we face and the need to unite against it; if it works, great - we have our spokesman.  If it doesn't, then we simply have the straightforward task of  discrediting him and claiming that he was not speaking on our behalf.  We lose virtually nothing, with everything to gain."

They discussed it for a while longer, the few remaining objections dealt with one by one.  Soon enough, the general consensus was reached, and they called Hieron back in to brief him for his five minutes of galactic fame.

- - - - -

Idly Hieron wondered if the chair had been chosen specifically to make him uncomfortable during the address.  It had a spring that was determined to gouge him in painful places no matter how many times he shifted position, and the cushion felt like it had been sat on so many times as to compress it into something more closely resembling stone than fabric.  The setting was deliberately a few stages shy of haphazard, so as to look official without giving the impression of the great and good making declarations from their ivory tower.  The room was virtually bare but for the chair he sat upon, the camera before him, and the desk in between.  Behind him upon the wall was painted the official seal of the Earth States Commonwealth; it had been decided that it was under their banner that the speech would be made.

He saw the countdown to record, and tried very hard not to think of how many people were going to see what he was about to say.  The red light came on, and the director's arm came down, pointing at him.  He inhaled deeply, and began.  "Citizens of Earth, and of the galaxy.  My name is Hieron Tomac, and I am speaking to you today on behalf of the Earth States Commonwealth, and a joint venture of seven of the galaxy's major corporations.  Not long ago, I led a sortie comprised of military forces from each of these corporations against a major pirate base on Korpi in the Xylon system, following years of unchecked aggression and rejections of diplomacy. During the assault, both we and the pirates were attacked by an unidentified craft, or array." He paused to take a breath, and let what he had just said sink in to his imagined audience.

"It approached at sub-light speeds greater than those of which our own craft are capable - approximately eight kilometres per second. It stopped above the planet, and unleashed a kind of energy weapon upon the surface, focusing, it seems, upon the pirate base there. Within a few minutes, the planet's surface was heated past the point of human tolerance, and despite our efforts to stop the assault, all upon the planet perished in the heat. Our own attempts to engage the array were met with overwhelming retaliation. It is through luck alone that I sit here to address you now." The pain was welling in his chest, a dark pool of agony threatening to rise and consume him. Tears started from his eyes, but he did not let them fall.

"One hundred and forty six members of the combined corporate militias, security forces, and mercenaries, were killed. It is estimated that at least twice that number of pirates met their end in the same attack. Whatever this thing is, or whoever they are, they do not discriminate between lawbreakers and citizens; they are not interested in talking to us; they do not fear us. Quite simply, ladies and gentlemen, they are the greatest threat humanity has ever faced, and face them we must. Following the example set by the seven corporations, the Earth States Commonwealth has agreed to join forces under a single banner to resist the advance of this hostile array."

"I am here before you to not only provide this information which has been kept from you, but to issue this appeal: no matter on which side of the law you currently lie, no matter what you have done in the past, no matter the price on your head, this day you are offered a complete pardon - if you will join with us. The most important thing we must do now is unite - together, whatever our differences, we are stronger. We can return to fight amongst ourselves another day, if that is all you wish to do. But for now, I beg you to put aside your petty, pointless rivalries and juvenile bickering, and stand with us to hold the line against this terrible threat. Divided, we stand no chance. United, we can win through. We *will* win through."

The red light was extinguished, and as he stood, the sound of a single pair of hands applauding came from behind the camera, revealed to be Kiah when he emerged into view. He was beaming from ear to ear, and seemed as if he was about to embrace Hieron, until the pilot-come-spokesman took a step back unconsciously. A look of profound hurt whipped across the face of the white-haired man for the briefest of moments before he regained control of himself and turned his approach into a firm handshake.

"You did it, you magnificent bastard," he laughed. "We'll have them eating out of your hand in no time. I hope you enjoyed yourself?" he didn't wait for a reply before continuing. "Because there's going to be plenty more speeches to come if we're going to pull this off. But I'm telling you, every one of them is going to be adorning the pages of the history books for centuries to come and do you know why?" This time he actually did pause long enough for Hieron to make a shrugged shake of his head. "Because we'll be the ones writing them, Hieron my good man. This is the beginning of something immense - something *epoch*-making."

Sure enough, there were more speeches to come. Hieron had been adopted as the official spokesperson for whatever the group was that was in charge - he was still not clear on who was calling the shots any more. He supposed the public probably felt the same way, and made a mental note to bring that up in the next meeting; they needed a name for this new group who controlled not only the nations of Earth but a significant majority of the rest of the galaxy too.

- - - - -

It was already dark by the time Neri turned onto Thom's street in Englewood Cliffs, New Jersey. The monorail had been strangely quiet, the few passengers keeping to themselves and generally reading a news sheet or examining a PDA. It was like everyone had retreated into their own private worlds to process the news from last month's public address by Hieron Tomac; she privately admitted that she had an urge to do the same thing. But that would not be the act of a responsible citizen, so here she was, walking through the silent deserted streets of suburban Jersey.

She was not looking forward to tonight's emergency meeting; Max would be gloating every available second, and might even try to take over the leadership of the group again. She wasn't sure she could take a second meeting in his cramped, malodorous, litter-strewn Bronx apartment. That she had narrowly avoided being mugged on her way back to the monorail probably had not helped her opinion of the neighbourhood. So it was with not a little trepidation that she finished her ascent of the inclined driveway and raised her hand to pull the cord for the door chime.

The maid led her to the drawing room, where they customarily held their meetings, and Neri thanked her as she left. The room was completely silent, and she groaned inwardly; Max had annoyed them into speechlessness once again, it seemed. She took her seat and looked around at her fellow freethinkers - Thom, with his lustrously dark skin and bright eyes, dressed as usual in his ostentatious smoking jacket; Cerydwyn, for once not fixing her arresting emerald eyes on the shabby Max, but instead gazing at the table before her; Max himself seemed paused in his habitual act of stroking his dull brown shrub of a beard, mouth gaping slightly. They barely seemed to notice her as she made herself comfortable, removing her short leather jacket and pink knitted hat. She straightened her glasses and looked around again, waiting for someone to say something.

"Guys?" she eventually offered, becoming genuinely concerned. "What's up?" It took a while, but eventually Cerydwyn turned to face her, pushing a thick lock of red hair out of her face.

"Did you see that?" she asked, cryptically.

"See what?" Neri asked, perplexed. Cerydwyn gestured vaguely at the television, and Neri guessed at what she meant. "Oh, there's been another broadcast? I didn't catch it, my PDA's on the flake. What did he say this time?"

"He announced a new era for humanity," Thom informed her, his words humming out as if he were in a trance. "The fucking calendar, man. It's been millennia since anyone fucked with the fucking calendar."

"Calendar?" Neri repeated, becoming only more confused by the second. "What's he talking about?" she asked Cerydwyn, hoping for more sense. Max was still frozen in place.

"New way of marking years," Cerydwyn replied distractedly. "As of today, we are no longer in the year we were yesterday - this is the First Year of Unity." The capital initials were audible in her voice.

"Unity?" Neri parroted, wishing someone would start making sense. "What's Unity?" It was Max who provided her with the answer she wanted, and yet the last one she wanted to hear.

"From today onward, all human endeavours will be governed by the Council of Unity - the six representatives of the Earth States Commonwealth, seven corporate heads, and one Church official. We all now belong to a single nation called Unity, with a single Navy to enforce its will; and to mark this great occasion they have reset the calendar back to one. The First Year of Unity has just begun."

# Chapter 7

As the months went by, Hieron continued to be placed in front of the camera to make some speech or another, usually extolling the virtues of cooperation and the need for everyone to do their part so that humanity might be made as strong as possible.  He was told that, on the whole, the message was being received well; people were scared, and seemed quite willing to submit to the authority they had asserted.  For the citizens of Earth, very little had changed - the Earth States Commonwealth was still more or less in charge of them, and had apparently been merely expanded to include some of the more powerful corporations.  They were well used to living under a single, centralised government.

It was beyond Earth that their problems began; while the more developed systems closer to Earth were fairly accepting of the regime change, having lived under the control of one or more corporations - and by extension, the Earth States Commonwealth - for most if not all of their lives.  The outlier systems were another matter entirely.  Those were populated for the most part by people who had only recently settled there through corporate colony schemes, and who had done so, on the whole, to escape the centralisation of power elsewhere.  These citizens objected in varying degrees to the new government, feeling that their modest amount of independence was being taken from them.

The worst, however, were the wildcat colonies on the fringes of inhabited space.  These were systems where the corporations had only extended a tentative toehold, perhaps with a scouting colony here, a temporary base there.  The people who had settled out on the fringe were those who desired independence at any cost, generally attempting to subsist on the land in whatever way they were able. A great proportion of these colonies had a history of being outright hostile to the corporate militias, and this antagonistic stance was only increased with the declaration of Unity.

However, as their planets and systems in general did not include any significant mining or farming infrastructure, they were not as important to Unity as those systems closer to the core, and to Earth. A majority of the conferences around the table centred on taking control of the various raw materials available to them, and how best to go about centralising the allocation and distribution of those resources. Hieron found those meetings quite horrifically dull, but he knew that this was the business of government, and tried to pay as much attention as he could muster.

He was still generally unsure of his role within what was now being referred to as the Council of Unity. They referred to him as their spokesman, but he also retained his role as an advisor second only to General Leetman; though they tried to consult him more than the General, he made sure that in matters of grand military tactics he always deferred to her judgement as he had vowed to do during the battle above the skies of Korpi. He had seen virtually nothing of the technician, Klaira Destri, who had come to him in his darkest moment and given him the verbal shakedown he had needed. He was not sure why he sometimes spent most of an hour trying to locate her, or what he would say to her if he succeeded. He told himself he just wanted to thank her for providing some perspective, but whenever he did, he knew it wasn't quite all that he wanted to say - but was unable to fill in the gaps.

Kiah was getting friendlier toward Hieron, too - often accompanying him on the walk back to his quarters after a session of the Council. The white-haired man still made him a little uncomfortable, but on the whole seemed to be pleasant enough. They even joked together a few times, usually at the expense of fellow Council members, and when they did so Hieron realised how long it had been since he had laughed last. Despite not sharing his views, he found the spiritual man's presence oddly comforting. On a few rare occasions, Kiah would join him for a cup of coffee in his quarters, and they would talk about Unity policy; Hieron was still unwilling to assert himself in the Council, and found that ideas he raised in those occasional meetings with Kiah somehow made their way onto the agenda in the next session around the conference table.

72

The military preparations were well underway; every shipyard under their control was busy churning out Hornets, Lightnings, Valkyries, and various other designs - all with fresh paint jobs displaying the blue trident crest of Unity. A scouting drone had been sent to Xylon to gather whatever intelligence it could about the array; the pictures it took of the surface of Korpi were broadcast to the galaxy, and support for Unity increased. But the most valuable outcome of that mission was the recovery of data from the pirates' unmanned buoy, apparently overlooked by the array in its business of destruction. What it showed was that the array did not, on fact, use hyperspace travel to go from place to place; their top speed recorded by the buoy was close to light speed, but not surpassing it. The buoy also provided the last known trajectory of the array as it exited the system. These two pieces of information together gave the Council a likely time and place of the array's next encounter with humanity - ten years and two months, in the Tortuga system. A two-year expedition was set up to seed the space approaching the Tortuga system with sensor buoys, as an early- warning system. Considering the speeds of which the array was capable, it might give them half an hour's warning at the most.

The next order of business was to fortify the Tortuga system with a significant military presence so as to be ready when second contact finally arrived. The problem was that the primary inhabitable moon in the system was already heavily fortified, an independent colony determined to stay that way. It was declared a priority to neutralise the threat, and the first aggressive sortie of the Unity Navy entered its primary planning stage; meanwhile, the people of Tortuga were bombarded with calls to reason, to unite with the rest of humanity against the alien threat. They were given the most graphic information that could be found to persuade them, including a roll of those killed in the last encounter with the array, and footage shot by the scouting drone of the surface of Korpi. Black lumps on the images were dubiously identified as the charred remains of soldiers and families, though there was no way to be sure of the veracity of those labels.

- - - - -

The miners of Galapagos were, on the whole, a tolerant group of people. They lived on the outer edges of inhabited space in the Galactic East, on a planet that was mostly rock and metal. Their food was almost entirely imported, except what meager rations they were able to grow in hydroponic greenhouses, and water was similarly scarce, coming primarily from enormous vapourisers which attempted to harvest as much as possible from what humidity there was in the atmosphere. Sometimes, when circumstances were particularly adverse, they relied solely on the waste recycling plant to provide them with the water they needed. The weather on Galapagos was mild and uneventful, the scenery bland and uninteresting, the recreation facilities best described as limited and improvised. On the whole, however, the miners were content with their lot; most were serving a contract of twenty years with a very attractive pension waiting for them at the conclusion. In short, it took a lot to upset them; they were used to hardship, and did not feel hard done by.

Thus is came as something of a surprise when Sari Chodhu came home to her partner, in the foulest mood she had experienced since her belligerent teenage years. Not knowing how to react to this unprecedented anger, Ophie withdrew to the corner of the room until Sari had stopped banging crockery around and rattling the cutlery as if it had offended her.

"Sari honey, what's wrong?" she finally ventured. Sari hung her head, without turning to face her partner, and sighed.

"Plans have changed," she replied gratingly through her teeth.

"What do you mean, changed?" Ophie asked her, confused. She wasn't aware they had had any plans that night, or for the next week for that matter - at least, not anything in particular.

"The new government has commandeered our mining facility and has promised to pay us more." This served only to confuse Ophie even more.

"Well that's good, isn't it? And we know the ore is going to be put to good use in the war effort -" she stopped short as Sari spun to fix her with a fiery glare. Never before had she seen her partner's eyes flash like that, and it scared her a little. Sari was barely stronger than her, physically, but her difficult childhood had made her a fighter, whereas Ophie had always been the shy one in her family. Her older brother had always outshone her.

"We get more money per hour now," Sari continued, barely restraining her voice that wanted to shout. "But the pension's gone. Hell, the whole fucking *retirement* is gone!" Ophie felt her face grow white as Sari's meaning was made clear. No pension. No retirement. No end to their work on Galapagos.

"But they can't do that," she objected. "We have contracts signed and witnessed, they can't just cancel them and say tough luck."

"Well that's odd," Sari snapped back, "because that's exactly what they're fucking doing!" She punctuated the end of her sentence by smashing her fist down on a pile of plates, the top three of which shattered leaving the fourth cracked but intact. The sudden shock of it made Ophie jump violently, and she felt like she was about to cry. It wasn't her fault, after all; why should Sari be mad at her? She felt the tears in her eyes, and wished more than ever before that she wasn't so weak.

Sari's eyes softened slightly, however, when she saw how upset Ophie had become, and she stepped in to embrace her fiercely. "I'm sorry Ophie, I really am," the sincerity was as strong in her voice as the anger had been moments before. "I wanted us to have a real future together when we were through here, but now everything has been taken from us without so much as an apology. How are we ever going to buy a house, or raise a child, while we're stuck here mining this wretched fucking ore for the rest of our lives?" The edge had come back to her voice, but was now tinged with the despair that lay beneath.

Ophie sat down heavily on the couch to let the news sink in. They had all heard the news, of course - the campaign against the pirates, the alien array, and the ascent of the new galactic government. But somehow, it had all seemed so far away; they were not used to thinking of themselves as part of the wider galaxy, as part of a vast human society. The aliens were coming from the Galactic South West, on the opposite side of the galaxy from Galapagos. When Unity was declared, nobody had thought that it would truly affect them on any real level - one government was much the same as another when all you're doing is cutting ore from the solid rock. The reality of the situation was starting to become clear.

- - - - -

Garion wanted for little; his work on his father's farm was rewarded with plenty of food, and a small allowance that he was putting aside for his next trip into town. He was never short of love, either; even when he was in trouble with his family for some reason, he could go to the next farm where the elderly matriarch of the house would dote on him for hours at a time. All in all, he felt he had it good - though his experience of life was admittedly limited to his eleven years as a farmer's son and nothing more. He had heard stories, though, of what lay beyond the farm, and even beyond the city - up in the sky, people flew from one planet to another, meeting new people and trading with them. But from what he had heard, that life was dangerous; he preferred to stay safe and warm in his bed by the fire, and content himself with merely dreaming about being a pilot or a trader.

That evening, after a long day of chores around the yard, he stepped up to the front door and was about to go in when he heard his father's voice. He was angry, a sound which Garion had learned to avoid. He listened for a while, to find out if he was talking about his son. If so, then he would lay low at the old lady's place for the night. His father had never struck him, but every time he was angry it seemed like he would, and Garion did not wish to be there when the mood finally took him. He took a step away from the door when he heard something smash; it definitely sounded like a time to hide at the other farm house. But then he heard his father's voice again, screaming at the top of his lungs. "*BASTARDS!*" he exclaimed. Garion decided it wasn't something he had done, and tentatively pushed at the door, swinging it inwards.

His father stood facing away from him, shoulders hunched as he leaned heavily on the kitchen dresser. The shards of a bowl littered the terracotta tiled floor, and Garion's mother stood patiently but prudently out of the way in the doorway to the next room. Her expression gave little away as to the reason for his father's outburst, but it clearly showed that she was concerned about something other than the broken crockery. She saw Garion enter, and raised a hand slightly, palm out, to tell him that he was better off staying where he was for the time being. Garion obeyed silently.

"They can't do this!" his father continued in a raised voice just shy of his previous scream. "What are we going to sell at the market? Our arrangement with Galactic Agriculture has always been that the land would be used half for their crops, and half for our own. This will leave us with barely enough to feed ourselves, let alone leave us enough to sell on the market! Ninety percent! Ninety *fucking* percent!" His fist amplified the obscenity, striking the dresser on which he was leaning.

"We will survive," Garion's mother told him quietly. "It will not be easy, but the ten percent will allow us to get by without starving at least."

"I know that, Bett," he replied, more quietly now. "But that doesn't make this fair. Not by a long chalk. You know what else they're doing?" He glanced over at her, to catch the shake of her head. "Replacing Canter and his men. Bringing in their shiny new Navy to keep the peace here." The word 'Navy' was spat like a curse. His large, muscular back heaved with an enormous sigh, and Garion's mother beckoned him to her, guiding him into the next room and out of harm's way. She followed him to the large, comfortable sofa on which they had spent many blissful evenings of his life, playing games before the fire. She knelt before him and looked into his eyes, her own large, deep hazel eyes damp with suppressed sorrow.

"My dear son," she began, her voice steady despite her obvious distress. "I'm afraid we're about to begin some rather difficult times. The new government has decided to take most of what we produce here, instead of the half that the corporation used to take. This won't leave us with much, but we will get by."

"Why are they taking it?" Garion asked, ever the curious boy.

"Well there are some bad things happening in the galaxy at the moment, son" she replied. "People are preparing for a very large battle that we absolutely have to win. Our food is being taken so that everyone can be sure of having enough."

"Well that's good isn't it?" he had always been taught that giving to others was a good thing to do, particularly those in need.

"Yes my boy, it is good" his mother assured him. "But it's going to make things very difficult. Your father and I will not be able to put on those big meals we have for special occasions, and I'm afraid we can no longer afford to give you an allowance. We will give you whatever we can, whenever we can, but it won't be a regular thing any more." Garion nodded quietly. He would miss his trips into town.

- - - - -

The mood was ugly on Arbiter Station. The head of the security forces had barricaded himself in his office and was quivering behind his desk with a laser shotgun aimed shakily at the door. Beyond, the corridors of the security facility were eerily quiet, completely deserted for the first time since they had been built. The only sound was the faint echo of a distant cacophony, rattling through the halls from the recreational areas. Far from having control of the situation, he had been abandoned by the vast majority of his officers who had now joined the mob that had begun an hour ago in the cafeteria.

It was no mystery what had set them off: he had made the announcement himself after Administrator Fuzi had chosen to delegate the responsibility. The Administrator had not been heard from since, and Chief Dester had his suspicions that Fuzi had chosen that moment to take a short impromptu holiday; certainly one of the VIP shuttles was missing. So Dester had taken a deep breath, and made the announcement over the tannoy, choosing to read mostly from the official dispatch from the Unity Council. He was not in the best of moods as it was; the new arrangements were almost as hard on him as they were on the rest of the workers on Arbiter Station, but his sense of duty kept him - albeit nervously - at his post.

Not so the rest of the station. The announcement was received with shouts of disbelief at first, which Dester had heard from his office; then the real reaction began. A few known troublemakers banded together and broke the security on the weapons locker, possibly with aid from members of Dester's security team. Then they started shooting at everything they knew would not explode back at them, including a couple of security officers who had been loyal and foolish enough to stand up to the mob. He was not sure which was more frightening: the heavily armed and extremely annoyed mob, or the fact that he had just been informed that a Unity security detail was about to dock at the primary airlock.

On the opposite flank of Arbiter Station, a dropship bearing the blue trident of Unity glided gracefully toward the airlock. Within, a dozen soldiers stood ready, weapons and kit checked and rechecked; it was their first real operation as a unit, and nerves were fraying left and right. They knew their training would see them through, and all of them had seen combat before within the corporate militias, private security forces, or even pirate groups. They were among the best that Unity had to offer, at least for the time being. The briefing had been simple - stand by while the announcement was made, and if trouble was reported move in immediately to secure the facility. Lethal force had been authorised but not encouraged, and while opposition was to be expected, it was predicted to be light and disorganised.

Finally the ship shook slightly as contact was made with the airlock, and a solid seal obtained. The green light flashed on, and the door swung open into the station, releasing the confined soldiers in a quick but orderly stream. At the first fork they split into two teams, moving off to secure the various zones of the station just as they had been ordered several hours previously. Everything went like clockwork until Alpha team reported hard contact. Bravo went to assist, outflanking the hostiles by approaching the cafeteria from the opposite direction. Shouts filled the room, echoing from the walls as the Unity troops called for the surrender of weapons, and were met with shouts of defiance and rage. It was not clear who truly fired the fatal shot, but the official reports later told that a refinery worker had aimed a Mark Nine laser rifle at a member of Bravo team and fired, hitting the woman in the eye and killing her instantly. This was followed, the report claimed, by an extended fire fight during which every Arbiter worker in the cafeteria - a head count put the number at twenty seven - was killed.

Bravo carried their comrade back to the dropship while Alpha continued on mission, sweeping through the extensive facility searching for any further signs of hostility. Room after room was cleared until they came to the residential section; intelligence told them that over two hundred people lived and worked on the station, and every one of them had quarters in that one section. Alpha waited for Bravo to complete their own sweep of the station before advancing in; no chances were to be taken.

Finally, Bravo arrived at their location, reporting hard contact with only seven hostiles, and successful neutralisation of all such targets. That meant that there were well over one hundred and fifty people in the residential section, many of them armed but not all. Alpha Leader instructed one of his team to slice into the central computer, connecting their radio directly to the speakers spaced regularly throughout the station. He used it to inform those within the residential area that Unity had sent them to ensure the safety of Arbiter Station and that any within who still bore arms were to show themselves in the central courtyard and discard their weapons. This was met with complete silence from within, and so Alpha and Bravo advanced carefully into the plaza.

The courtyard closely resembled one that one might expect to find on the surface of a planet; grass and plants grew in a small park in the centre, flanked by two-storey structures and well-kept paths. The only difference was that there was no sky - merely a high ceiling decorated with large, soft lights. Nobody was in sight when the Unity soldiers entered, and they stuck to the walls on either side, two members of each squad detaching themselves from the group to stand watch while the rest of their comrades cleared each building as they passed. The second time this happened, there was a laser shot from the second storey a few buildings down, and a shout of "hard contact!", then the courtyard erupted in laser fire. Both sentries of each squad were down in seconds, with no cover to speak of.

What followed was a desperate fight with an inevitable conclusion. The former Arbiter workers were armed and numerous, but their opponents were better equipped and trained for just such occasions. Twenty women, four men, and eighteen children survived. Unity lost no more soldiers than the five that had already fallen.

# Chapter 8

"I don't call over one hundred and fifty dead workers an acceptable loss!" Hieron shouted across the table at Dang Zhou, who sat blithely nibbling on a muffin after having delivered his interpretation of the disaster at Arbiter Station. "Not to mention the soldiers we lost - it's fortunate that the two were merely wounded. What are we going to do about this?" He looked interrogatively around the table at the other members of the Council.

"It's all in hand dear boy," Balfour patronisingly reassured him. "New workers are being shipped in from Earth and we should have the station back up to full production capacity in a couple of weeks. The team we sent in has been reinforced with fresh recruits, and have been offered the appropriate counselling. I don't know what more we can do."

Hieron could do little but gape at the round man, smiling blandly through his cartoon moustache as if he truly had no notion of why their spokesman might be so upset. Finally he found his voice. "I meant, what are we doing to prevent this sort of thing happening again? Are we going to have another Arbiter Station every time we give people some bad news about the necessary cutbacks?"

"Of course not," Gendson scoffed. "Why, we've already broken it to a dozen colonies that they'll be making less money for a while, and this is the first time any of them turned nasty. Well," he added after a moment's thought, "nasty enough that so many folk died anyhow. I hear there were a couple of riots here an' there but they got put down real peaceful like."

"Does 'peaceful' mean nobody dead, no Unity soldiers dead, or everybody dead?" Hieron retorted hotly, anger flashing from his eyes.

"Now there's no need to be facetious," a mollifying voice interjected just as Gendson was about to grind out a reply from between his teeth. The voice belonged to Ari Zack, who had of late taken on the role of peacekeeper around the conference table. It was a job that kept her very busy indeed; it seemed that the Council of Unity was unable to disagree without raising their voices, and, more times than not, unable to agree. Gendson was about to turn his scorn upon her, probably accompanied by some horrifically sexist platitude, but Hieron beat him to it.

"You're absolutely right, Ms Zack," he told her in a calm and level voice. "A massacre or two is hardly something to get worked up over."

"Might I remind you, Mr Tomac," Dang Zhou interjected, "that you are an advisor here? However much we might value your advice, and your services as our spokesman, you do not have a vote around this table. Your powers of persuasion are useful in the public eye, but in this Council there is no place for rhetoric." He poured enough derision into that last word so as to make it quite clear how much value he truly placed on Hieron's contributions.

Hieron looked him square in the eye, bowed mockingly, and left the room. He muttered to himself all the way back to his quarters, and continued to do so as he entered, using a few choice curses for both Zhou and Gendson in particular.

"Couldn't agree more, my friend," Kiah told him, smiling from his seat at Hieron's table. Sat across from the white-haired man was the tall, slim form of General Leetman, sipping a cup of coffee in her customarily restrained manner. Hieron idly wondered if she ever let her hair down and enjoyed herself, and what that would look like. Then he got back to wondering why these two were in his quarters uninvited, and why he had failed to notice their absence at the Council. The latter was easily answered by how little attention and respect they were normally accorded in that room. Kiah allowed him his moment of surprise before continuing. "That's why we're here," he explained. "We think it might be a good idea to get cooler heads together to answer the questions that we all know need answering but won't get answered by that bunch of stuffed suits." He motioned for Hieron to join them at the table, who did so.

"I have taken the liberty of designing a new training program for our soldiers which should see them performing more efficiently in just four weeks, and attaining the expertise of elite troops in two years." Leetman, businesslike as always, laid an indicative hand on the file in front of her. "At the least, the initial training should give them the necessary conflict resolution skills the lack of which was, I believe, the root cause of the massacre on Arbiter Station. It is not unusual for regular soldiers to react to the deaths of their comrades in an extreme way, particularly if that unit has not seen much combat together before. This training will solve most of the problem, and keeping the troops active on short peacekeeping missions will solve the rest."

"Which brings me to the second point," Kiah said. "There are still a significant number of settlements in the outlier systems which have yet to submit to Unity's rule, ignoring the gracious offer of amnesty and choosing instead to remain independent. Normally I would say 'good for them', but there isn't a single human-occupied planet that we can do without - it's all or nothing, and everyone has to do their part. Tortuga in particular," he added. "We need to fortify the system of Tortuga as our primary forward defensive line - it's our best guess at the location of the next encounter with the array. But there is still a significant pirate presence in the system that needs to be pacified - I hope peacefully by the powers of our persuasion. If it has to come to force of arms, however, we must be willing to commit to that course too."

"Tortuga is too strong at the moment," Leetman told him, "to offer any guarantees of success, particularly with our fresh troops. I have made a recommendation to Mr Sicarius that we continue our peaceful negotiations with the colony while our troops are trained, and send them on smaller sorties against more minor targets."

"There are many planets," Kiah took over, "even closer to the core, where defiant colonies have sprung up in remote parts, far from the primary settlement and spaceport. Most are minor, a few makeshift buildings and farms, that sort of thing; but there are a few that cause us concern, and even the majority of the smaller bases are significantly militant in their attitude. Needless to say, our offer of amnesty has been roundly ignored by all of those that are still presently active. These will form the perfect crucible in which to temper our troops together into a single, united force."

"What about more peaceful options?" Hieron could not help but ask. He knew the need for the absolute unity of humanity, and knew it better than most; but part of him still blanched at the reality of making it happen.

"Of course we are still exploring those options fully," Kiah assured him. "We want a minimum of violence to occur in this transitional period. An independent base will only be targeted by the Navy if it has rejected all of our attempts at a diplomatic resolution. Only the most stubborn will be subject to the use of force," he reassured him.

"We have some very interesting research regarding the peaceful options, in fact," Leetman told him, shuffling the folders in front of her and indicating another. "It seems that those colonies least inclined to insurrection such as we saw at Arbiter Station are those with a strong affiliation to the Church." This surprised Hieron for a moment, but started to make more sense the more he thought about it - was the Church of Intentionality not concerned most intimately with assuring people that everything happened for a reason, and that cooperation was the way to ensure the greatest happiness?

"You want to persuade more people to join your Church, don't you?" he guessed, and Kiah's smile told him everything he needed to know.

"It makes sense, Hieron," he told him. "If we can get some missionaries out to these rebellious colonies and persuade them that Unity is a necessary part of the Great Destiny, it's quite possible that we can avoid any more unnecessary bloodshed. Reams of research has been done - even apart from this latest stuff -" he indicated the folder on the table, "which clearly shows that citizens are more content and less likely to complain if they describe themselves as members of the Church. In an ideal galaxy, every citizen would be a member - and true unity could be attained."

"Would the Council approve that action?" Leetman enquired. "I know most are members of the Church but there is a long-standing tradition of keeping spiritual matters separate from the political."

"And look where that's got us," Kiah argued, then broke into one of his unsettling smiles. "No, they'll agree. I have something of an ace up my sleeve."

- - - - -

The next meeting of the Progressive Policy Debate Forum was far more lively than the last, Cerydwyn thought happily, though considering the stunned silence that had prevailed at that meeting, it was hardly a difficult achievement. They sat around Thom's dining table deep in conversation, sometimes more than one person speaking at once but never raising their voices. They all knew something had to be done; Unity was a fundamental threat to the freedom they saw as standing at the core of their way of life, and they had no doubt that the alien threat was just what Max had said it was - a fiction, and the perfect excuse for tyranny.

The actions of the independent colonies were occasionally inexcusable. Cerydwyn and her friends in the group knew this, but always stressed to anyone who would listen that one need not support their actions in order to support their cause. Private citizens had no less right to stake a claim to unowned extrasolar real estate than did corporations, and yet the former were treated like criminals when they tried to do so. Now that Unity was in the picture, the hopes of the small outlier independent colonies to govern themselves were looking more and more likely to be extinguished. It was even discouraging Cerydwyn from her regular fantasy of flying away to a paradise island somewhere on the edges of inhabited space with Max, and setting up their own self-sufficient idea of heaven.

When he had arrived an hour ago, Max had brought fresh intelligence from his anonymous source - the Church was making its own move, seeking to increase the number of agents it had active in the galaxy by persuading Unity to use them as some kind of diplomatic peacekeeping negotiators. Naturally this would involve attempts to convert to their religion the colonies that Unity saw as hostile. As staunch opponents of established religion, the Progressive Policy Debate Forum did not receive this news well. It was just the sort of insidious tactic that could work - not only in its stated objective of pacifying the independent colonies, but also in its obvious covert objective of increasing the Church's power base.

Two main objectives began to emerge from their deliberations - uncover the alien hoax for what it was, and gather more intelligence regarding the Church's plans for Unity. How they were going to do either one of these remained something of a mystery, however, until Max hesitantly offered a solution.

"My source could be of some help" he admitted, after visibly grappling with the idea for some time. "We might be able to gain access to the data stored on Hieron Tomac's black box." They collectively gaped at him for a moment while that information was digested.

"What? How? Who is this source?" They all clamoured, in different permutations of the same words.

"I really cannot tell you," he sighed. "As much as I trust you all, I cannot risk exposing my source to the kind of danger he or she would be in if it were known where I was getting this information - or even that I was getting it at all. Suffice it to say that my source will be, or is, in a position to gain access to the black box recording of the events above Korpi. We will know for sure, then, what really happened."

"How are we going to decrypt the information once we have it?" Thom asked, uncharacteristically curious about what Max had to say; perhaps he was finally taking the poor man seriously, thought Cerydwyn.

"I have a friend who works in software engineering," Neri answered, smiling wryly. "He's an old boyfriend, actually. I'm sure he'd be willing to do me a favour like this if I gave him the impression I might sleep with him." They all paused momentarily as they tried to reconcile that last sentence with their habitual perception of Neri: small, shy, retiring, and a bit of a geek.

"All very well," Thom said, breaking the spell, "but what do we do then? Once we've go this evidence in our possession, what do we do with it?"

Max smiled the smile that made Cerydwyn's stomach tingle. "We tell everyone," he said simply.

- - - - -

The Primus of the Church of Intentionality arrived at Alamo Station just a few days after Hieron's clandestine meeting with Kiah and the General. Awe and deference marked his arrival, the majority of personnel being members of the Church and the others being generally overwhelmed by his celebrity. He wore his customary Italian suit, holding his head high as he slowly made his way down the exit ramp of the luxury shuttle. He formally greeted the Council of Unity, arrayed in the hangar to receive him, and promptly went to shut himself in a private conference with Kiah. The corporate heads and Commonwealth dignitaries did their best not to look offended by this, and for the most part failed.

The conference was so private that even the Primus' acolyte, the girl who was perpetually present at his side, was not permitted to accompany them. Instead, she made her way to their quarters to prepare them for the Church leader's arrival and approval. Very few people noticed her do this, however, as she was very used to remaining unnoticed even when surrounded by people. One of the few who did spot her moving around quiet and unassuming was a third-level station technician, who decided to follow her for a reason she could not fathom.

Klaira had been avoiding Hieron ever since the day she had visited him in his quarters and given him a piece of her mind when all she had intended to do was offer comfort and understanding. She had decided that this was because she was embarrassed by her outburst, but in her more honest moments she admitted to herself that it was also coloured by the discomfort she felt every time she saw him. She had spotted him on a number of occasions since their last meeting, usually striding purposefully through the corridors toward or away from the conference room where he seemed to spend most of his time. She wanted to approach him, and apologise, or at least to simply see how he was; but every time she tried, something stopped her.

Now, however, she was following a girl who looked to be in her mid-teens, walking quietly and unobtrusively through the corridors of the station, for some unknown, subconsciously assigned reason. Perhaps it was simply fascination with the Primus; though she did not know anything about the role this girl played in the Church, she was clearly close to the old man and that surrounded her with a powerful mystique - something only compounded by her discreet meanderings through Alamo Station.

Klaira was not surprised when she saw the girl disappear into the VIP quarters that had been set aside for the use of the Primus; what had made her think that the girl might have something to hide? She was about to return to her duties when the door opened again and the girl came back out, walking straight toward her. Klaira had a momentary, irrational urge to run away, but by the time she had dismissed the thought it was too late anyway. The girl stood before her, solemn brown eyes gazing impassively at her own; Klaira noted that they were the same height, which was unusual as most were far taller than her in her experience. The girl's hair fell straight, a lustrous curtain of black falling from her head. She reached out a perfect hand and touched it to Klaira's cheek.

"Hieron needs to talk to you," she told Klaira, sparking off a mental torrent of confusion and questions begetting questions. She wanted to ask them all to the girl with the wise eyes, but somehow when she tried, all she could manage was an incoherent splutter. The girl smiled and walked away, leaving Klaira alone with her tumbling thoughts. After a minute or more of remaining rigidly immobile, she set off down the corridor toward Hieron's quarters. She followed the command implicit in the girl's statement as if it were a command from the Creator itself; and who was to say that it was not?

Before long, she had come upon his door, and reached for the intercom. After three chimes there had been no answer; he was either not inside, or deeply asleep, or simply not accepting callers. She considered ringing again, and speaking through the intercom to let him know it was her, but was interrupted by a deep voice from behind her.

"Looking for me, Technician Destri?" Hieron inquired, the faintest, barely detectable tinge of humour in his tone. She stammered, unsure of what to say and trying to use several possible excuses for her presence at once. He took pity on her and invited her inside. He poured them each a cup of coffee, and they sat at his table in silence for a while, neither certain what to say. Finally Hieron broke the silence. "What brings you here again? I thought you were avoiding me."

"I was, but-" Klaira brought herself up short, realising how bad that admission had sounded. "That is, I was trying to give you some space. I felt bad about yelling at you, and I didn't -" she hung her head and sighed deeply, cursing her awkwardness. Time to start over. "I came here because I thought you might need to talk," she finished, finally.

"About what?" he asked, demonstrating his typically male propensity to intentionally miss the point. She sighed again.

"I don't know," she admitted. "I just thought that perhaps you might need to talk about how you've been getting on since I -- since our last talk." He shrugged, infuriating her further. "So you're fine now?" she snapped, wondering why she always had to end up raising her voice when she was talking to him. "Just like that, I give you a little perspective and the massacre at Korpi doesn't bother you any more? The dead faces have stopped haunting your dreams?" She knew by the look in his eyes that she had gone too far, but had no idea how to take it back.

"No, they're still there," he said quietly, gazing distantly into his coffee. "But as you say, you gave me some perspective. So if you're just here to yell me out of offing myself again, I can save you the bother."

"Oh, Hieron, that's not what I came here to do at all," she told him, reaching out to lift his chin so he met her gaze. "I'm sorry I always end up shouting at you; you just frustrate me. I know we've only met a few times, but every time I feel us click - then you clam up and refuse to show me what's really going on in your head." His eyes were rimmed with tears, and she had to choke back her own, born of the knowledge that she had caused him pain. His hand raised from the table to meet hers still at his chin. She felt his warm skin against hers, and a thousand possibilities raced through her mind. Then he was around the table and kissing her, tongue gently pushing into her mouth as they explored each other, each revelling in the closeness of the moment.

Her uniform and his suit fell piece by piece to the floor, creating a soft irregular path to the cot. While normally cramped, hard, and unwelcoming, the small military-issue bed was to become heaven for the next few hours as they explored their mutual passion, both emotional and physical. Neither had the opportunity or inclination to think about what was happening, or why, or whether it was a good idea; lost in the moment, they both did their best to make the moment last as long as they could.

# Part Three
## Chapter 9

The Council, with only a gentle push from Kiah and the Primus, eventually approved the plan to send missionaries to the colonies that had not yet submitted to Unity rule. The pragmatics of the idea were not lost on them; any colony that could be persuaded to join them through words rather than force of arms was the kind of double victory they needed. Building the kind of military force that they believed they would need - both to destroy the array and to keep the peace throughout the colonies - was turning out to be even more expensive than they had calculated. The latter problem, in particular, was proving to be far more troublesome than predicted by all but the most pessimistic analysis.

The core worlds had made very little fuss about the recent shift in the balance of power, with the exception of Earth, where the population was so high that the law of averages meant virtually every possible opinion would be represented by someone. The core systems, though, were generally wealthier and longer-established, with cities rather than colonies, and several settlements on each planet rather than the one or two which became the standard toward the fringes. The people were different, too - the farther out from the galactic centre, the more the frontier mentality made itself known. Some planets were little better than crime dens, the local thugs, having long chased off any local industry, now lived from the proceeds of raids on traders, corporations, and other colonies. Needless to say, these fringe worlds had greeted the change of regime less quietly.

Tortuga was the worst of these. Shortly after the planet had been discovered by scout ships, a wildcat colony had sprung up, a small but determined group of people intent on making a life for themselves in the new world. They did well - too well, in fact, and by the time the colony had reached ten thousand settlers, their *ad hoc* government structure had become rotten through with corruption. It became the galaxy's primary center for black market goods, being far enough from the core worlds to avoid any kind of regulation or law enforcement. The history of Tortuga from that point onward consisted of little else but turf wars between the various crime gangs who had moved in for a slice of the profit. Eventually a kind of equilibrium settled over the troubled colony, and they began to bother the trade lanes more than they fought amongst themselves.

Needless to say, it was going to take a lot more than preaching to remove the obstacle of Tortuga from Unity's path to galactic peace. Even the Open Information Campaign they had begun shortly after the battle in Xylon seemed to be being ignored by the Tortugans; the analysts hired by the Council suggested that this was probably due to a lack of faith in the veracity of the claims. In short, few if any of the people on Tortuga believed that aliens were responsible for the assault on Korpi. The possibility was raised more than once of letting them find out for themselves, and taking the extra time to fortify a system closer to Earth, but each time this idea was shouted down by a rare majority in the Council. Nobody wanted any more ground lost to the array.

Finally, after two difficult years of preparation, training, and planning, the assault on Tortuga was ready to be launched. Nobody had ever seen a fleet of the same size before, nor even one half as large; they gathered in the space around Alamo Station, slowly manoeuvring into formation. The calculations had been made to ensure that all the ships arrived at their destination as close in space and time as safely possible; there had been some significant advances made in hyperspace navigation computer technology in the years since Unity's founding, with Carter Technologies leading the way. After much wrangling among the Council, Hieron was finally awarded command of a wing of TA-77 Polecats, the latest generation of fighter from Tranquility Aerospace.

In all, two hundred ships would fly to meet the Tortugans in battle; while most were fighters, many old Lightnings and Hornets picking what was likely to be their final fight, there were a great many capital ships as well. No fewer than twenty Valkyries formed the indomitable core of the fleet, though even the Valkyrie's great, sleek fuselage was eclipsed by the new pride of Liberty Shipyards, the LS-100 Mastodon. With a crew of three hundred and seventy eight, four fighter bays, and more ordnance than was found on the average space station, it could probably have won the battle on its own. But no chances were being taken this time; now that humanity was united, cooperation was made far simpler; certainly the corporate heads still bickered, but when their products were the property of Unity rather than their own companies, it made decisions far easier to take. There was not a ship in the fleet, nor even an escape pod, that did not bear the blue trident symbol of Unity.

Hieron sat in the seat of his Polecat, hand on the throttle and awaiting the order to join the fleet. Apprehension filled his thoughts with the darkest possibilities in what was to come, but he pushed it back. The fleet had a commander, and for once it was not him; all he had to do was follow orders, pass them on, and keep his wingmen alive. He looked to his left, out at the bustling hangar of Alamo Station, and wondered if he would be seeing it again; it had become his home for the last two years or more, the only one he had known since leaving Earth and what had remained of his life there. His eyes were drawn to one figure in the hangar who was not a part of the bustle, a uniformed person who stood and stared sadly at the departing fighters. He knew what she was thinking, because he was thinking the same about her. Ever since their unexpected liaison two years ago, he and Klaira had become closer, sharing everything together and stealing moments of intimacy whenever they could. The feeling was a new one to Hieron, but now he was experiencing the other side of the coin, and what happened when there was a very real possibility that he might lose someone close to him. That feeling was distinctly not new, and he greeted it like an unsettling, unwelcome, old friend.

The order came, and he led his wing of four other Polecats out into the void to take their place in the great mass of ships. The Mastodon, named the UNS Concord, had already begun the jump to hyperspace a few hours ago, and as Hieron's wing settled into their assigned places, the twenty Valkyries joined it. Only the Hornets and Polecats, ten wings of five each, remained; the Lightnings and Tercels were being carried in the fighter bays of the larger craft. Being of a similar mass, the remaining ships were to make the jump to hyperspace at the same time, and the minutes dragged by as systems were checked and rechecked. Finally the moment arrived, and Hieron sent a message of good luck over the comm to the rest of his wing just before contact was lost as they entered hyperspace. It was a lonely place to spend so much time, and was the main reason so many would-be trader pilots simply found that they were not cut out for space travel - at least not in such small ships. When you had a crew, or could at least move around, it was far easier to remain sane in hyperspace.

After almost an hour of nothing but the black of hyperspace beyond the canopy, the computer beeped a warning that the scheduled exit from hyperspace was drawing near. He shifted all of his muscles one by one, settling into position ready for the tense action to come. There was the usual moment of peculiar disorientation as the objects at the destination - ships, planets, the star - were at once very far and yet very near to him. Then he was flying with his Polecats beside him, adjusting their formation to swing in behind the Concord's port stern. The eeriness of silence that had preceded the Battle of Korpi was thankfully absent, as the Tortugans knew very well what was coming and when. A large fleet, backed up by several weapons platforms, awaited the Unity ships. They flew to meet them.

- - - - -

Klaira walked the halls and corridors of the station, assisting with the preparations for the fleet's return; every last scrap of cargo had been removed from the hangars to make way for the repair equipment and triage areas. Intelligence suggested that the pirate base on Tortuga was fortified by half a dozen weapons platforms, and their fleet consisted of approximately one hundred ships. This meant that Unity's fleet would outnumber the pirates' by around two to one - not counting the fact that Unity had a greater number of capital ships. Good odds indeed, but no chances were being taken.

A ground assault had been ruled out early on in the planning stage; another disaster like Korpi would simply destroy confidence in Unity's ability to deal with rebellions, and they would have countless more on their hands before they could recover. The reasoning was that the vast majority of the pirates would be manning the fleet and the weapons platforms in orbit, so attacking the settlement itself became a low priority. The crime bosses, however, were not expected to join the fight; they were in for a surprise, though, as the UNS Concord would dispatch a ten-strong team of operatives to the surface via drop pods - their primary objective being to cut the head from the snake.

Her confidence in the battle plan as Hieron had told it to her, however, could not diminish the worry that gnawed constantly at her nerves. She narrowly avoided a disciplinary hearing when she very nearly snapped at her superior, a short bespectacled jobsworth called Herring. He was not the sort to think about his orders when carrying them out, nor the sort to forgive the slightest insult. She took a quick break to cool off, and had to fight the urge to walk the familiar route to Hieron's quarters, instead taking a circuitous route through the long, gleaming, bustling corridors.

A flash of black hair in the distance made her heart race; there was something mystical about the Primus' young acolyte, and in the two years they had been staying at the station, Klaira had seen her perhaps twice, always in the distance. She wanted to ask her so many questions, and thank her for what she saw as the girl's part in uniting her with Hieron. But every time she tried to follow her, the black hair would disappear into a crowd, or around a corner, not to be seen for another age. This time would be different, Klaira decided. Even if the girl disappeared, she would keep looking until she found her.

She took off at a half-run down the corridor, the black of the girl's hair a beacon at fifty paces. Sure enough, it soon disappeared behind a tall uniformed man with blonde hair, and by the time she was past him the girl had gone altogether. There was only one way she could have logically gone, though, as the other direction was a weapons locker; Klaira jogged on, truly unsure of what she would do if and when she finally caught up to the young acolyte. She decided to thank her first, considering that to be the most important thing and also thinking that such a courteous start might convince the girl to stick around a little longer and answer her questions.

Another flash of black in the distance made her pick up the pace; it seemed like the girl was running too, remaining fifty paces away every time Klaira caught sight of her. The chase had take n on such a strange, otherworldly quality that it took a few minutes before Klaira started thinking about the direction they were headed. The living quarters, and therefore the girl's room in the VIP suite she shared with the Primus, were behind them, as were the Council room and the main hangars. So what was in front of them, and why had she picked that direction? Logic struggled with mysticism in her mind as she tried to find an answer but kept coming up against the thought that the girl was simply an unfathomable mystery.

The main section's escape pods were ahead, she remembered. But why would the girl want to use one of those? Perhaps she was going to the canteen? But Klaira had never seen her in the canteen, and if that were the answer, why would she run there? So not the canteen; what else was in this direction? Secure storage, the bar, turret control for that section... Was that where she was going? To the turrets, so she could shoot a ship? No, that made no sense. As Klaira rounded a corner, however, her question was answered for her as she saw the door to secure storage slide shut. The girl was nowhere to be seen.

Her technician's access code had no hope of opening that door, but it was also the only way in or out of the room. The girl had to come out eventually, so Klaira decided to wait for her in the corridor which, in contrast to the adjoining ones, was virtually free of traffic. The few people who did pass paid her no attention as she loitered outside the sealed door, trying her best to look nonchalant as if she were supposed to be there, rather than at her post in the hangar. Finally, the door slid open to reveal the girl standing inside, clad in a plain white robe with a simple cloth satchel crossed over one shoulder. Her eyes went momentarily wide as she saw Klaira standing there, but her accustomed air of casual mystery was quickly restored. She opened her mouth to speak, but Klaira interrupted before she had a chance to excuse herself and hurry off down the corridor again.

"Excuse me, miss" she began. "I just wanted to thank you for what happened the last time we spoke; Hieron and I have fallen in love thanks to that meeting you prompted two years ago. I guess it's true what Kiah says - sometimes when the universe is trying to get something to happen, it needs a little helping hand. You're going to make a wonderful Primus one day," she smiled. The girl smiled back, a ray of sunlight in the artificially-lit corridor.

"You're most welcome," she said, every syllable a melody. "I do so hate to be rude, but I am in something of a hurry at the moment. The Primus and I are planning to leave for Earth as soon as the fleet returns, and there are still many preparations to make for the journey." She took a step to the side of Klaira as she spoke, and the technician realised that this was all she would get out of the girl - two conversations in as many years. She smiled politely, and wished the young girl well on her trip back home.

- - - - -

95

There were so many ships in the space above Tortuga that at times it seemed there was more of them than there was space between them. Hieron found that it made navigation a little more interesting, to say the least. But the battle was going in their favour, and the Polecats were acquitting themselves very well indeed - to the point that he had even stopped missing his old Hornet. The TA-77s were more responsive to throttle, pitch, and roll, and that manoeuvrability coupled with their armaments made them fearsome opponents. There were more than a few pirates who were finding that out the hard way.

Still, as well as things were going, he could not help but be curious about the larger picture; his only communication with the *Concord* consisted of receiving his orders and acknowledging them. He was desperate to know what the tactical overview looked like, and to have news of the team sent to the surface; it had been his idea, raised by Kiah in the Council, and thus he felt responsible for the ten soldiers in the drop pods. He thought he had caught a glimpse of their tiny craft streaking toward the surface shortly after he had arrived in the system, but there was no way to be sure. One of the advantages of the pods' design was that they were too small to show up on scanners, and unless one was within a few hundred metres or so, the naked eye could not pick them out either.

After the first ten minutes of intermittent panic, he had set his own scanner to maximum range so that he did not get anxious every time the computer announced a fresh contact. The array was not due to reach the system for another eight years, but his paranoia told him that that was an estimate only, based on their severely limited experience of the array's behaviour. The brute fact was that they were not, and could not possibly be, certain of anything with regards to the aliens. He was continually forcing back memories of Korpi, and he thanked whatever fate there might be that the planets did not look overly similar. Korpi had been a lush, Earthlike world with vast primordial forests and immense green oceans; Tortuga bore more similarity to Mars, a predominantly brown, rocky planet with water but very little plant life. The colony's immense oxygen-generating tanks could be seen from orbit.

As he swung his Polecat about to chase after a small formation of Tercels and sent his wing to harass one of the four Tortugan Valkyries, he decided he had had enough, and opened a channel to the *Firebird*, the nearest Unity Valkyrie and incidentally the one commanded by an old acquaintance. "Fleck, this is Hieron."

"Commander Fleck to you, asshole," came the response, though he could hear her smiling through the words. "What do you want? Don't know if you've noticed but we're a little busy - there's some kind of battle going on."

"Sorry to bother you *Commander*, but could you give me a read on the status of the Predator team?"

"The status of the what?" she asked as he dodged to port and took a Tercel by surprise; it was the last mistake that pilot would make.

"The Predator team - the special forces we sent to the surface," he clarified for her. It seemed that the name had not gone much farther than the walls of the Council room.

"Predators," she responded flatly. "That's real original. How did you come up with that? Hours spent hunched over an encyclopedia?"

"Something like that," he replied, clipping the wing off a second pirate fighter and sending it spinning wildly out of control. "Got a read for me?"

"They're fine," she reported. "Objective neutralised and awaiting extraction. No friendly casualties. And you owe me one, Tomac."

"Perpetually, Commander," he smiled as he killed the comm link to the *Firebird*. The third and final Tercel of the former formation met its end under a withering stream of fire from his cannons, and he pitched back to join his wing in assaulting the pirate Valkyrie. His mind felt free of a terrible burden, and he threw himself into the combat with renewed vigour, dancing between the ships and laser fire, and sending missile after missile into the beleaguered capital ship. Before long, the starboard nacelle came away and a chain reaction in her propulsion made short work of dismantling the vessel from the inside out.

The Tortugan pirates were beaten, and they must have known it as surely as the Unity fleet did; but they had nowhere to run, so stood their ground, defiantly responding to every call for surrender with increasingly offensive obscenities. The last of their weapons platforms succumbed to the long-range hail of heavy fire from the *Concord*, and one by one the rebel fleet was dealt with by the swarms of Unity fighters. The last to be destroyed was a particularly tenacious Hornet who, despite having fought to safe jump range from the planet, refused to run. Three Lightnings fell to her lasers before Hieron's wing of Polecats moved in for the kill, leaving only debris and a floating corpse to join the cloud of orbital detritus. The Battle of Tortuga was over.

# Chapter 10

Max was fairly certain that he had never been so nervous before in his entire life. He sat on the cheap, thin mattress which in turn sat, with far too much room to spare, upon the bare metal frame in the motel room a few miles from Lake Nipigon. It was his first visit to Canada, and he was not enjoying it; quite aside from his nerves, it was unbearably cold, and there was no civilisation to speak of. Even the coffee was barbaric - thick, gritty, and far too dark for his taste. The two small milk sachets he had managed to locate hardly made it paler, let alone palatable. All of this he tolerated, however, for two reasons: first, the future of a free humanity was at stake; second, and more importantly, Gaia was meeting him there.

He leapt to the window for the third time that hour as he heard a car glide by outside. This one, however, pulled into the car park and a small, slight, dark haired, and achingly familiar figure stepped out. He bounded to what passed for the bathroom, and inspected himself; hair tied back just as she liked it, beard trimmed and combed, no remains of dinner anywhere to be found. Just as he decided that he was probably presentable enough, there was a light knock on the door that set his heart pounding even more heavily in his chest. He tried to remain calm, and crossed to the front of the room, taking a deep breath before pulling the door open.

She was even more beautiful than he remembered, his memory aided by inadequate holo-images he had made sure to capture the last time they had been together. Her hair was blacker, her skin smoother, her eyes deeper, and her smile utterly heartbreaking. They gazed at each other for a few moments before she leapt at him, throwing her tiny arms around his neck and nearly knocking him from his feet. He managed to remain upright and kicked the door shut behind her, carrying her limpet-like to the bed where they sat and held each other close, wordlessly, for what seemed like forever. Finally he separated her from his chest, and began to ask her something, but she put a finger to his lips, reaching into the satchel she carried with her always. From it she drew a small black hard drive, used to transport data from one system to another.

"Just like you said," she told him, smiling. "I transferred all the data onto this drive, and replaced the flight recorder back into secure storage. Nobody knows it's gone," she added.

"That's great, Gaia," he told her. "Really, really amazingly great in fact. But I was just going to ask if you were alright - you've had a long journey from Alamo Station, and it must have been stressful carrying this cargo." His eyes were filled with concern, and they were met with slight surprise in hers. She was still not used to having people concerned for her wellbeing, but rather being either invisible, or a tool, or a vessel in which people poured their knowledge and beliefs. He wanted so much to free her from that life, to let her choose her own destiny instead of have it dictated to her - but every time he had brought it up in the past it had led to an uncomfortable distance between them. Her destiny was the most important thing in the world to her, and the idea that it might not be already laid out before her seemed to be profoundly upsetting.

"I'm fine, Max," she said, uncertain in this unfamiliar conversational territory but apparently recalling his previous instructions of how such exchanges were expected to proceed. "It has been stressful thinking about avoiding detection, but knowing that I am doing the will of the universe has lent me strength and confidence. The people must be shown the truth, whatever that might be." Her last sentence was a verbatim repetition of what he had said at their last meeting, more than two years past.

They would inevitably ask where he had got the information; they might even doubt that it was genuine. But as long as he had blood and breath in his body, he would never reveal that his source was none other than the Primus' acolyte. To do so would almost certainly make her the next in a long and lengthening line of victims sacrificed to this new, grand destiny they called Unity. He held her to him, feeling her soft, light heartbeat through her plain robe. That would never, ever happen, he swore to himself for the fifty-first time that day.

- - - - -

"So what now?" Klaira asked him as they lay in their post-coital glow on the cramped bunk. "Now that the Battle is done, I mean."

"Well I hate to sound like a cliché," Hieron began, "but the war is far from over. Rebellions are still springing up across the galaxy, and although this defeat has weakened the criminal element considerably, I doubt we have seen the end of this thing yet." He squeezed her closer to him, kissing her head as he noticed the unease that had settled over her. "But as for the big picture," he continued, "Tortuga is going to be fortified with four heavily armed stations, to act as launch posts for the fleet that will be stationed there from now on. When that array finally arrives, we will be ready for it."

"I suppose," she replied distractedly. "But why do we have to spend so much time attacking our own people?" The question took him by surprise, and he fumbled for a response that was not simply a paraphrasing of one of his public address speeches.

"They're not our own people, K," he said, finally. "They have had every opportunity to become our own people, but they choose instead to set themselves apart, and live only thinking of their own survival. Any defiance is a threat to Unity - and we absolutely must be united when the array comes back. It's unite or perish."

"Is that what you tell the rebel colonies?" she retorted.

"That's not what I meant and you know it," he chided her. "Right now, our survival depends on cooperation. We can't do this without all of humanity backing us up. If the array gets here and finds us divided -"

"I know, honey, I know," she reassured him, taking his large hand between hers. "I just wish there was another way."

"We're exploring every alternative first," he told her. "Nobody's rushing in guns blazing without a thought for diplomacy."

"I suppose you're right," she said, mollified. They lay there in silence for the next hour or more, before it was time for Klaira's shift in the hangar. A lot of ships still needed attention, and the station technicians had their work cut out for them.

- - - - -

What was he going to do? The bitch had ruined everything - not just his hopes and ambitions, that was old news. Now she had gone ahead and scuppered his most carefully-laid plans with her meddling. It was simply intolerable! He took a deep breath, calming himself as much as he could. There would be a way to salvage the situation. There always was. In this case as with many more, however, it was not at all obvious.

Kiah paced in his quarters, as was his habit when agitated. Gaia was proving she was still capable of being a damned nuisance, and may in fact have been improving as she got older. He had hoped that Hieron's relationship with that technician woman would be a simple flash in the pan, a fiery, passionate romance that would burn itself out quickly without damaging his carefully laid plans. So much for that vain hope, he thought to himself. The woman was proving to be quite the pacifist, and her whispering her sweet misguided nothings in Hieron's ear would only serve to confuse him.

But what to do? If he managed to remove her from the picture, Gaia would likely just replace her with another. Anger rose inside him at the very thought of the black haired girl, just two years his junior and yet the reason he had been passed over for selection as the acolyte of the Primus. If it weren't for her, he would be the acolyte now, next in line for the Primus' seat at the head of the Church of Intentionality. And he would do a far better job of it than she would; in fact, removing her would be in the best interests of the Church as a whole.

There was no doubt - he had to deal with Gaia first; by far the more dangerous endeavour, but one which would give him far more satisfaction. A shuttle accident, maybe. No, she never travelled alone by shuttle - the Primus would be with her. Poison? Perhaps, but delivery method was always fraught with complications. A straightforward murder, then? Perhaps by shooting? No. The first thing they would look for was motive, and the first person they would question was him. But wait a minute. Who were 'they', exactly? Police, answerable to the Earth States Commonwealth, answerable to Unity? And who was he if not the puppet master of the Unity Council? If he could not get away with murder, who could? The plan began to form. He would need a third party to carry out the act, to give him at least the veneer of deniability. And he wanted to be there, to tell her why she was being killed.

Just as the first smile in hours touched his pale face, the door chime sounded and he opened it to find one of the Predators there. They were proving very useful indeed, and seemed able to perform virtually any feat of stealth in the book - and a few that had been redacted from the book. He beckoned the woman inside, ignoring the urge to check the corridor beyond for witnesses. The Predators did not take kindly to insults.

"What do you have for me?" he asked eagerly. She would not have bothered him with a personal visit unless it was of the utmost interest and importance.

"The acolyte girl has a lover," the soldier reported tersely, and went on to describe what had happened at a remote motel in the frozen hinterlands of Ontario. The smile on Kiah's face returned, and widened as he learned of the perfect reason for the legitimate termination of his greatest enemy. Gaia was a traitor, to the Church, the Primus, and to Unity. Right there and then, he formed the plan for her removal; the Predators would again prove themselves most useful indeed, and he could move on to considering the problem of the technician. Her faith would be a useful handle, if he was careful about exactly how he pulled.

- - - - -

Thom had never seen Max in this mood before. He had never been the most upbeat person in the world, by a long chalk, but at today's meeting he seemed like he had recently had his heart broken. He had presented the drive to Neri with barely any fanfare, after the group had all braced themselves for the incessant gloating that they had considered to be inevitable. But instead, the bearded man had simply entered, made himself a coffee, drowned it in milk, and handed Neri the drive. He now sat staring into his coffee as usual, but somehow more melancholy.

"Did somebody release another uncomplimentary biography of Marx?" Thom teased, trying to lighten the mood, or at least get him to talk. But Max failed to react at all, let alone take the bait and rail against his perennial tormentor. Finally, Thom had had enough, and was about to genuinely enquire after Max's wellbeing, but Cerydwyn rather predictably beat him to it. Max just shrugged and continued to stare at his coffee flavoured milk.

Neri, meanwhile, had linked the drive to her PDA and was apparently establishing a connection to her friend the software engineer so that he could crack the encryption for them. That he was willing to do so without any questions asked whatsoever was a testament either to Neri's power over him, or his obsession with encryption systems. Considering the kinds of geeks he had known in the computing industry, it could easily be either one of those possibilities. The group waited in the uncomfortable silence while Neri's anonymous friend pitted his skills against the military encryption algorithms. Twice Cerydwyn attempted to prise a word or two out of the nigh-catatonic Max, and twice he replied with the barest shrug of his thick shoulders.

An hour passed, by the end of which Cerydwyn had resolved to simply sit with her arms folded on the table in front of her, her head resting on them, and her eyes fixed on the melancholy Max. Neri was still deep in conversation with her friend while he did his job, and Thom had taken to doodling aliens on the jotter pad he carried with him. Finally, Neri let out a little whoop, which Thom interpreted as 'job done', demonstrating great optimism in spite of the fact that the previous two whoops had signified big news on the kawaii forum she was browsing. This time, she looked up from her PDA to smile around at the rest of the group.

"We're in," she declared, and even Max raised his head at that. The evidence was theirs, and they would finally discover the truth behind the propaganda.

"So what happened at Korpi two years ago?" Thom asked her.

"Well, if I patch this in to your house's mainframe, I should be able to give us a look at the scanner readout from the moment Hieron launched his Hornet. It seems that the battle was already well underway by that point, too - the fleets are fully engaged." She tapped a few commands, and the two-metre television screen set into the room's west wall lit up with a representation of sensor data gathered from the Korpi system at the time of the battle. There was nothing strange about it, if one discounted the fact that it was a virtually unprecedented moment of cooperation on the part of supposedly rival corporations. Certainly there was no array of the sort described by Hieron in his public addresses.

"Do you have the audio logs from the comm channels?" Thom asked her, thinking it might help make more sense of the dancing coloured lights on the screen. She nodded, and tapped away again for a few moments. Voices started coming from the speakers, narrating the engagement. They could hardly help but wince every time a pilot's voice was cut short, knowing what that meant, and more often than not seeing the coloured icon turn to grey and disappear. They grew more and more confident that there was no array, when a voice came from the speakers that they recognised as the ensign operating the scanners aboard the *Hariasa*.

"Black Leader be advised," the ensign said, tension only too clear, "fresh contact bearing two seven eight from our current course. Four hundred clicks and closing fast." From that point, they listened and watched with grim fascination as everything Hieron had told them and the rest of humanity appeared to be indisputably corroborated before their eyes. As the voices coming through the comm systems became more frightened and insistent, Neri shut down the replay. Nobody objected; there was no need to watch any more, and the audio was unsettling to say the least.

"Well I don't think there's a lot we can say to that," Thom broke the silence, finally. "We were wrong, and Unity might just be right. If this thing is still out there, we need to prepare some kind of defence."

"How do we know this data is even genuine?" Cerydwyn asked, anticipating Max's unspoken question as the bearded man sat even more dejectedly at the table, still staring at his cup of cold coffee.

"We know," Neri assured her. "My friend has... experience of this kind of encryption, and he said that the data is genuine. There's a time stamp on it which would be almost impossible to fake."

"*Almost* impossible?" Cerydwyn pushed.

"Let's not grasp at straws here," Thom interrupted. "We need to accept that this data is the genuine article, and deal with the reality that that revelation presents."

"Well do we know for sure that the array was of alien origin?" Cerydwyn asked. "I mean, it could have been an experimental new weapon that got out of hand in its first live test."

"I don't think that makes a lot of sense," Neri argued. "It travels faster than any human creation ever has, deploys a weapon that we have nothing even close to, and kills seemingly indiscriminately. It makes no sense to suppose that it is anything other than what they say it is."

"So the question remains," Thom said, standing authoritatively, "what do we do with this information? Share it with the world and tell them something they have already been told? Use it to win over those who doubt what Unity has told them? We certainly know plenty of people who fit into that last category." He looked to Neri and Cerydwyn, who seemed to have no suggestions. Max, however, raised his head to look straight at Thom. There was a strange pain behind his eyes.

"So the aliens are real," he said. "It makes no difference in the end, because they are still using this massacre as an excuse to establish and exercise supreme centralised control of the whole of humanity. People in the outlier colonies are still suffering in their mines and on their farms, Unity soldiers are still being deployed to quell any challenge to their power. And you mark my words - when this array is finally destroyed, and the threat is ended, not one of those in the highest positions of power will willingly choose to stand down. By that point it will be too late - humanity will have sacrificed its freedom once and for all, and the only hope of getting it back will lie in violent insurrection."

"So we do nothing?" Neri asked, a few long seconds into the silence left by Max's words. Thom sighed heavily.

"We do nothing about the black box," he said. "But Max is right. People do not give up power easily, and we all know the old adage about absolute power - which is the kind we're dealing with when it comes to the Council of Unity. Even if they have the purest of motives at the outset, there's no guarantee they will remain pure; in fact, if history is any witness at all, the opposite is guaranteed. So we prepare in whatever way we can, and continue to be vigilant. In the event that Unity retains absolute hegemony after the alien threat passes, then the revolution begins here, with us." He looked around the room at the others, who nodded grimly in agreement.

# Chapter 11

The ride from the spaceport would have been quicker on the monorail, Kiah mused as the car hovered at a junction heavy with traffic. But he had never been able to stand those things, and for some reason the thought of being that closely packed in with dozens of British accents made his skin crawl. Finally though, he arrived at his destination and stepped out to look upon the glory that was the central offices of the Church of Intentionality. They stood on the old site of Birmingham's Central Library, a monstrosity of a building that was torn down early in the twenty-first century to make way for the new Church headquarters. They gleamed in the morning sun, a sight to rival any of the greatest works of nature, and Kiah felt the familiar awe as he gazed upon the wonder of humanity's power and grace.

Victoria Square was quiet, the market stalls just setting up for the day before the crowds descended upon them. He waited by the fountain in the centre of the square, glancing up at the clock tower of the art gallery every few minutes. Right on schedule, at seven o'clock, the girl came walking down from the Church building to the market, a daily ritual that could be relied on like clockwork. He stepped out to meet her as she approached, smiling broadly. She stopped in her tracks upon seeing him.

"Gaia, my dear!" he greeted her cheerfully. "Beautiful morning isn't it?"

"What are you doing here Kiah?" she demanded with steel in her voice.

"I just wanted to let you know that you have failed, Gaia," he told her, still smiling as he closed the distance between them. "You have failed to break my plans, and you have failed to break me."

"What are you talking about?" she asked uncertainly, her steely tone wavering.

"Your little matchmaking game with Hieron," he answered. "Pairing him off with that weak, pacifist technician. Don't pretend you don't know what I'm talking about - the game is up, and you have lost spectacularly."

"I really have no idea what's going on in your paranoid mind, Kiah, but that thing with the technician happened entirely by accident - she happened to run into me while I was busy so I distracted her by telling her Hieron needed to speak to her. I had no idea the two of them even knew each other - let alone would be attracted to each other. Fate works in mysterious ways indeed, it would seem." She smiled a patronising smile at him and set his blood on fire; he wanted to seize her there and then, throttle her to death in the middle of the square. But that would be counterproductive. Instead, he forced a smile by reminding himself of the current situation.

"Well, your happy accident will soon be undone," he told her menacingly. "Thanks to your little stunt over in Canada -" at this she froze, all levity gone from her expression. "- I have gained a rather special dispensation from the Primus himself. I am to replace you as acolyte, effective immediately." She reacted surprisingly well, considering the fact that he had just effectively removed the single most defining fact of her existence. She stepped close to him, looking up with the raw hatred burning in her eyes.

"Do what you will, Sicarius," she growled from between gritted teeth. "I know enough to bury you three times over, and I've just been waiting for the day you would give me an excuse." He looked down at her dark eyes, wide with ire, and smiled.

"You know nothing that would harm me in the slightest," he told her.

"I know what you do in your quarters when you're all alone with your spy cameras," she whispered. "I know you spend a great amount of time watching Hieron's feed. Even when his little technician friend is at work."

His hands twitched into fists, and his arms desperately wanted to fly out to shut her up permanently, but he very carefully controlled himself, and after a deep breath he leaned down to whisper back. "*That* is why I am here." He checked his watch, and looked to the clock tower again. He nodded, and watched with great satisfaction as she crumpled to the hard, cold stone of the square, a small round burn at the nape of her neck.

The new acolyte to the Primus of the Church of Intentionality smiled a wide, triumphant smile. The Predators were indeed proving very useful.

- - - - -

News spread fast. Though the vast majority of humanity had no idea of her name, Gaia had been a familiar face to all from the newscasts of the Primus; an anonymous, pretty face who always seemed to be near to the old man. Those who had no idea supposed that she might well be his nurse, old as he was and certain to be prone to the maladies of that condition. But even those who knew what she was had no idea of who she was; an acolyte's life was entirely eclipsed by his or her role within the Church - doomed to be an apprentice, and nothing more, until the Primus was called to the next life.

A galaxy mourned, but they mourned as one mourned a distant relative, their grief tempered by the girl's anonymity, and the knowledge of her treason. She had attempted to breach security at Alamo Station with the objective of fomenting a rebellion against Unity and the Church, they were told. It was hard to have sympathy for someone with so little regard for the Great Destiny of humanity, but for a few days it was the chief topic of discussion around dinner tables throughout the inhabited worlds.

The Progressive Policy Debate Forum soon deduced that she had been Max's contact in the Church, and upon realising this they all rushed immediately to his New York apartment. If Unity knew about Gaia and what she had done, they might well know about Max and his involvement in her treason. Considering the rumours surrounding her rather impromptu method of execution, they wanted to ensure that Max was still safe. The three of them stood on the lobby of the apartment block where he lived, exchanging worried glances as the seconds ticked by. A minute passed following their first try of his buzzer, then another. They tried again, with no luck.

"OK," Neri said. "None of you are seeing what I'm doing right now." She took some small tools from her pocket and opened the panel on the door release. After a few moments of tapping and poking around while the others made sure nobody else was watching them, the communal door slid open and allowed them access to the apartments. They hurried through, up the six flights of stairs and along the sparsely-lit hallway to Max's door. Thom knocked loudly, all of them holding their breath to catch the slightest noise from inside. Not a sound came to their ears, and he knocked a second time, more insistently than the first.

After another thirty seconds of silence, he told them to stand back as he ran full force at the wooden door. He bounced off once, and a second time, but on the third attempt, the frame split and the door flew open to reveal Max's living room, the walls adorned with pictures of Karl Marx, Che Guevara, and Lenin, and quotes from the same people. The floor was strewn with papers and snack wrappers, the table in the centre littered with coffee cups that probably dated back several weeks. The curtains were drawn, lending a dark golden cast to the scene.

They took a door each, Thom checking the bathroom for the sake of modesty, Neri taking the kitchen, and Cerydwyn checked the bedroom. Thom was about to report that Max was nowhere to be seen in the bathroom - a fact for which he was quietly grateful - when Cerydwyn screamed. Neri and Thom shared a look across the living room, their hearts at once both sinking and racing, then they both hurried to join their friend in the bedroom. Neri immediately turned back around as soon as she saw what was in there, then after a moment's thought turned again to pull Cerydwyn's agonised face away and held her close as they cried together. Thom simply stared, numb and morbidly fascinated, at the corpse hanging from a hook in the ceiling.

Judging by the colour of his face, Max had probably been there a day or so. He hadn't begun to smell much yet - no more than he usually did, at least. There was a stool on its side a metre away, its most recent use only too clear. Thom walked forward a little to examine the body of his former friend, checking for laser burns, cuts, or anything else that might suggest foul play. He found nothing, but he did not let that stop him from considering the possibility that Max had been silenced permanently by Unity operatives. He would have liked that.

- - - - -

Klaira was inconsolable. The minute they had heard the news about Gaia's execution, she had collapsed in tears on the bed; it was news to Hieron that the two had even known each other. He had not himself spoken to the omnipresent black-haired girl, but he had received the distinct impression that Kiah did not trust her. Whether that meant that he himself should trust her, or distrust her, he had never been able to fathom. When Klaira had calmed down a little, she told him between sobs how the girl had sparked their first romantic encounter; she truly believed that Gaia had a gift for interpreting and carrying out the will of the universe. There was nothing he said that could make her stop crying, so he simply held her close until she drifted off to sleep.

He left her there and went in search of Kiah. He did not share her faith in the Great Destiny, but he knew that it was just this sort of situation in which faith could be a real help in getting her through. He found the new acolyte in his quarters, sat with two cups of coffee on the table in front of him. He smiled as he saw Hieron.

"Hieron, my friend," he greeted him. "I've been expecting you."

"So I see," Hieron replied, feeling the familiar unease at the warmth of the welcome he received from the white haired man. Nevertheless, he sat down opposite him and took the coffee gratefully. "I've come to ask you a favour, Kiah," he told him. "Klaira is taking the news of Gaia's death a little hard, and I know she has strong faith in the Great Destiny - so I was wondering if you could have a word with her, to you know -" he waved his hands in the air vaguely "- work your magic, make her feel better." Kiah smiled again.

"Well, it's not quite magic, my friend," he laughed. "But I would be only too glad to offer her the support she needs at this difficult time. Gaia's treachery came as a surprise to all of us, even the Primus Himself, who perceives the vagaries of our collective fate with greater clarity than anybody else. I myself cannot think what contribution it might make to the Great Destiny, but I have faith that there was a reason behind it. Perhaps I was destined to become acolyte," he added. Hieron smiled awkwardly, then thanked him for his help and left to return to the woman sleeping in his quarters.

Kiah reclined in his chair happily. This was going to be far easier than he had thought - a few of these so-called counselling sessions with the technician should convince her that everything he wanted to accomplish was in the best interests of humanity. He might even be able to persuade her that Hieron needed to do this alone; but that would have to be a secondary concern, and definitely required a great deal of subtlety and finesse. The most important thing in the short-term was to ensure that she stopped filling Hieron's mind with notions of peaceful resolutions attained at any cost, and an unthinking opposition to military action.

- - - - -

Meanwhile, the Council of Unity oversaw the fortification of the Tortuga system. Six large orbital platforms were constructed, each capable of launching a significant flotilla of ships, and each armed with four immense laser cannons. Research continued into more effective weapons, more manoeuvrable ships, and more powerful shields. The sensor readings from Hieron's flight recorder were pulled apart and examined in the minutest detail by experts all over the galaxy, searching for as much information as could be obtained regarding the array's terrible heat weapon. The few clear images captured by his onboard camera were scrutinised for any clues to the array's construction and possible weaknesses.

Rebellions continued to be courted by the Church, and put down firmly by the Navy when diplomacy failed. Hieron continued to address the citizens of Unity to stress the importance of cooperation and reinforce the threat that was approaching from the Galactic South West. Klaira and Hieron continued to grow closer, and though she had stopped urging him to keep the Unity Council on the straight and narrow track of diplomacy, her earlier admonishments stuck in his mind. Five years after the Battle of Tortuga, and seven after their initial liaison, they were married during a rare leisure visit to Earth. Hieron had the whole thing planned well in advance, proposing on an equatorial African beach at sunset and then informing the speechless technician that their wedding was in one week, and that it was exactly as she had always described her perfect wedding day.

Their happiness even managed to make the monotony of their day to day tasks seem bearable, and another two years flew past before things started to get interesting. According to the best estimates gained from the array's last known trajectory and velocity, they were expecting it to arrive in the Tortuga system within the year. The preparations were very nearly complete when Hieron had two very different pieces of news.

The first came early in that final year when, after nearly three years of blissful marriage, Klaira told him that she was expecting his son. He would later look back upon that day as the absolute happiest of his life; the worries of Tortuga seemed so distant as he sat on their shared bed, holding his wife tightly to him and grinning uncontrollably. He had never been a man who was forever dreaming of being a father, but now that he was going to be one, he could think of nothing that would make him so happy and complete as meeting his son and raising him.

The second piece of news was almost as exciting, though on a very different level. After decades of false starts and technical problems, Carter Technologies announced to the Unity Council that they were ready to begin field testing of an EEG chip. Implanted painlessly - and, if necessary, temporarily - under a pilot's skull, it would allow complete mental control of any given fighter craft, once the wireless connection was made. The technology had been around in various unworkable forms for a very long time, it seemed, but had never been a viable method of navigation until now. Preliminary tests were very positive indeed, and it was widely seen as just the edge they could use in fighting the array; the ability to dodge and weave from the paths of the drones and their continuous laser-like beams would be utterly invaluable. Coupled with the newer, more manoeuvrable ship designs, it gave them all hope that victory would be not only possible, but probable.

The bad news was that, as one of the Navy's most experienced pilots, Hieron was expected to have a direct hand in the final stages of testing the devices. He went for the procedure immediately after the Council session, and was informed that the chip now in his brain had already been calibrated to connect to the TA-77 Polecat he had flown in the Battle of Tortuga. As much as he wanted to spend all his time with his wife at that moment, he could not help but be somewhat excited by the prospect of testing the new technology. It would save lives in the thousands, particularly if it was ready for use by the time the array reached Tortuga.

Klaira was predictably morose at the news, though she grudgingly admitted that the technician in her was really quite excited by the prospect of the technology. They had a passionate final night together before he left for the training, which was to take place in the Hephaestus system, on and around a rocky moon that Godsforge Munitions used for all its weapons testing. Due to the untested nature of the systems, the four Polecats were to be taken to the system in the fighter bays of the *Firebird*. It would take the better part of a day to make the journey, and the training was scheduled to take four weeks, so as to ensure complete confidence in - and complete familiarity with - the capabilities of the chip.

It was a tearful goodbye, as Klaira held her face tight against Hieron's chest as if she was never going to let go. He reminded her it was only for a month, and that he would be back in plenty of time to support her through the rest of the pregnancy. There was no way he was going to let anything prevent him from being at her side when their son arrived, and he had told her so several times a day each day since he had discovered he was to be sent on this training. He had never felt this way about any departure before in his life; even when he was leaving for Tortuga, he had not been this completely desperate to return just as soon as he could.

Kiah watched as the tearful couple exchanged farewells in the privacy of their shared quarters, and momentarily wondered if his plan would work, and if it was the right thing to do. He quickly dismissed these thoughts as weak-minded, however; the Great Destiny would not be achieved by its facilitators having second thoughts. It was clear enough that as things stood, Hieron was not going to be the hero they needed him to be by the time the array reached Tortuga. It would take a significant change in his near future to set him back on the right path.

# Chapter 12

The first day of training had gone well, in general; though every one of them was an experienced pilot with endless hours clocked up behind the flight stick of one fighter or another, the new system was completely unfamiliar to them. So the first stage involved them simply floating in space, using the small attitude thrusters to maintain several different wide formations and trying not to bump into each other. It was, Hieron found, somehow both terribly complex and mind-numbingly boring at the same time. So it was that the four pilots gathered in the bar aboard the *Firebird* after the debriefing.

Hieron had not met any of the other three pilots before, but they were familiar faces from the station; sooner or later, you got used to the faces of everybody who worked there. One person in the bar with whom he was more familiar, though, was Commander Fleck, formerly of Frontline Fuels and now of the Unity Navy. The change had been good to her, her talent for command finally being acknowledged; there were rumours that she would not be commanding a Valkyrie for much longer, and that the *Concord* might just be her next assignment. Of course, being privy to the deliberations of the Unity Council, Hieron knew these rumours to have more than a grain of truth. But he was not at liberty to discuss it with Fleck, and to her credit she never asked him.

He raised his glass in her direction as she approached the group, and she smiled graciously, sitting down between him and the only female pilot of the group. "So, did you enjoy the floating exercises today?" she asked mockingly. "It must have been terribly taxing for you."

"No less taxing than sitting in a big chair giving orders," Hieron retorted, smiling.  They continued to gently mock each other, with the three other pilots happily joining in once they realised there was no malice in the words.  Then the conversation switched to the technology itself, and their honest and informal assessment of how it could perform.  Finally, as the night wore on, the heavier conversation topics surfaced - the array, the past, the big picture - and the other pilots excused themselves one at a time, leaving Hieron and Fleck alone to reminisce about that first ill-fated run against Juliano Station.

"Do you really believe in all this Great Destiny shit?" Fleck asked him finally.  He thought carefully before responding.

"My wife does," he told her "and I've got no problem with that.  I have no idea whether there's anything to it or not, and my wife has no problem with *that*.  We don't agree, but we don't disagree, and she knows not to go on about it.  It's not a perfect arrangement, but it works for us."

"Well I'm glad I'm not the only one who thinks the whole thing is a little far-fetched," Fleck smiled.  It was the first time she had smiled so genuinely at him, without the usual sarcastic or mocking caste to her face, and he was struck by how attractive she was when her eyes lit.

"I should be getting to bed," he declared, looking the clock on the wall above the bar.  "Long day of floating tomorrow."

"I hear they might actually let you turn the engines on," she smiled back, the familiar and friendly mocking smile returning to her face.

Sure enough, the lesson for the second day was the throttle.  It felt distinctly like they were back in boot camp, at their first lesson in how to be a pilot; it was a gruelling experience, but they gritted their teeth and stuck it out.  There would be time to learn acrobatics later, when the simple manoeuvres had become second nature and they were no longer a threat to themselves and each other.  They were all looking forward to the weapons testing scheduled in the final week, but accepted the need to get through the basics first.  They had all seen what could go wrong in live weapons tests, and none cared to experience or witness that again first hand.

The bar was a little more subdued that evening, with the novelty wearing off the training and the holiday atmosphere starting to dissipate rapidly.  Conversation tended toward more serious subjects,

116

such as the impending battle against the alien array. All of them knew they would be flying in that battle, probably heading a wing of Polecats each. They also knew only too well how many pilots had survived the last encounter with the array, and a respectful quiet fell over the table whenever Hieron spoke of the Battle of Korpi.

Despite the camaraderie of the gathering, Hieron was feeling alone. Whether it was the drink, the fact that his wife and child were on the other side of the galaxy, or the uncomfortable memories being stirred by the conversation, he was not sure. But they had only been talking for a little over two hours when he excused himself and retreated to his temporary quarters, where he opened a fresh bottle and poured himself a glass. The spirits were thankfully not chemically addictive, and the hangover the next morning was minimal; yet they were still pleasantly intoxicating, and he felt an unfamiliar desire to get as intoxicated as he could.

Another two hours later, he was well on his way to reaching that goal. The room was starting to rotate gently around him, and he went to sit on the bed for the sake of stability, holding on to the edge of the table and then the chair to support him on the way. He had been there, staring into his glass, for only a few minutes when the chime on the intercom for his door sounded. He threw a few handy items at the button for the door before one hit the right spot and the light of the corridor spilled in, revealing a silhouette of Vesta Fleck.

"Tomac, what the fuck are you doing?" she demanded as she entered. "This a healthy way to deal with your problems?" He shrugged, and she snatched his drink from his hand. "You got problems, I get it. But hiding away and drinking yourself into oblivion is not the way to deal with them." She knelt in front of him and looked sternly into his eyes. "We've been through some heavy shit together, you and me. I know I wasn't there for Korpi, but I know what you're going through right now. Probably better than anyone else. I know the only thing keeping you going for the last nine years or more has been that beautiful wife of yours, and now you're away from her you're alone, you're afraid, and you don't know how to cope." She put a hand on his shoulder, and he met her gaze with tears in his eyes. "Lean on me," she said. "Share with me."

- - - - -

117

Hieron had been gone for three days when Klaira sought out Kiah for a counselling session. She had been doing so for many years, ever since her mind was finally put at ease over the treason and execution of Gaia; now she was desolate over Hieron's absence and needed consoling. Kiah had proven a true friend to both Hieron and herself over the last nine years, and she found her talks with him both enlightening and uplifting. He had a talent for seeing the best in every situation - a talent she both admired and envied, and which made her seek him out whenever Hieron's soft spoken, laconic support was not quite enough to lift her spirits. Perhaps, she sometimes thought, it was because her husband had little faith in the Great Destiny and the innate wisdom of the universe. Whatever the reason, Kiah had become her closest friend and confidante.

"I share your sadness at your husband's absence," he told her, "but possibly not for the same reasons."

"What do you mean?" she asked, puzzled.

"Well it is only natural that you miss the man you love, the man you married. But my sorrow at this time comes from my knowledge of his fate." Klaira's face turned ashen, her worst fears written plain upon her small, delicate features. He held up a hand to stem the tide of grief about to wash over her. "Not death, dear lady," he assured her. "Hieron is not destined to die during this minor training exercise. But if you recall, he has a certain history with a woman named Vesta Fleck; they are old comrades back from the earliest days of our little cooperative endeavour. I regret to tell you that this history, combined with several other factors, leads them to form a liaison while away on this exercise." He paused and held her hand as the information sank in and she began to shake.

"You're certain of this?" she asked, her voice wavering. He nodded solemnly.

"I am afraid so, my dear. It is written quite clearly in the stars for those who know where to look."

"What should I do, Kiah?" she asked, tears standing in her eyes as she controlled herself with a great deal of effort. "I always thought it was my destiny to be his wife, and the mother of his child. What is my destiny now? To remain with him despite this, or to leave him?"

"I am afraid I cannot tell you," he said, head hanging. "The paths of your fate are not at all clear."

"Well maybe that's my answer then," she replied. "Maybe my path is unclear because this is where I cease to be a significant part of the Great Destiny. This is where I leave."

"Come now child," Kiah comforted her, unconsciously adopting the speech mannerisms of the Primus. "There is no such thing as an insignificant player in this great game; every tiniest role has the utmost importance to the Great Destiny. Even if you decide to sever your direct connection to Hieron's thread now, your fate will continue to influence and be influenced by the great tapestry of humanity. You will still have meaning, and what's more, you will have meaning of your own - not the reflected meaning of your husband. You need no longer be eclipsed by his seemingly more prominent fate, should you choose so."

She thanked him sincerely, still holding back the tears, and left for her quarters. Everything there reminded her of Hieron, and she knew then that she could not go on knowing what he had done. She collapsed in tears on the bed, and cried herself into a deep sleep, in which she dreamed of holding him close to her. But then Hieron cut the child from her belly and hid it from her, forcing her to spend the rest of her life searching the galaxy for her son.

She awoke in the morning with the dream fading from memory but the unease and melancholy it had left behind still strong in her mind. In silence, she packed her belongings into several bags and made for the main hangar. There was a shuttle leaving for Centauri IV later that day, and she boarded. It was three hours before the shuttle was due to depart, but nobody gave her a second glance while she sat in the passenger compartment, as if she was meant to be there. Perhaps she was, she mused to herself as the thrusters fired and she was taken away from Alamo Station, and Hieron, forever.

- - - - -

The training picked up after the fourth day, with the pilots becoming confident in their ability to control the ships with their thoughts alone. They started splitting their training between space flight and atmospheric flight above the moon's surface, the formations becoming tighter and the manoeuvres more complex. They performed evasive drills, with drones firing dummy ammunition at them to simulate various different types of weapons. Eventually, their own weapons were activated and they began to shoot back, but it was only on the second day of the weapons drills that they began to hit the targets reliably.

The socials in the *Firebird*'s bar had grown closer over the weeks of training, with the pilots learning to trust each other in the drills and that trust spilling over into their down time. This did not get in the way of a bit of friendly competition, however, and at the end of each day's training they would sit in the bar and compare scores. Burton, a pilot formerly of the Earth States Militia, was particularly consistent in his scores and rapidly became the man to beat during every exercise. Hieron did not know what the man's leadership skills were like, but he knew Burton would distinguish himself at Tortuga given the chance.

Tamaria, the single female pilot, had once been the brightest star of the New Hellas defence Fleet; her decorations spoke for themselves, and not one her fellow pilots failed to recognise that or be impressed. The New Hellas Fleet had been known as one of the most dangerous postings in the galaxy prior to Unity's ascent to power, perpetually at war with their neighbouring system, New Persia. Their squabbles were literally the stuff of legend, and to have a pilot so highly decorated from that world spoke not only of her ability to kill, but her ability to stay alive. Both would be utterly invaluable at Tortuga, and other pilots would naturally follow her - particularly those from New Hellas.

Finally, the third man of the group, Arno, was a relatively fresh recruit with only a year's service behind him. At the age of nineteen, Unity was virtually all he had ever known, and as such he made them all feel terribly old. But his talent was indisputable, and it was for that reason that he had been handpicked to participate in the groundbreaking training. He would not be given his own command at Tortuga, though; with no leadership experience, he would likely be assigned a Second position in one of the Polecat wings. Hieron was doing his best to lobby the Council to ensure that that wing would be his.

Fleck and some of the other Valkyrie crew had also taken to regularly joining the pilots for their habitual post-debriefing drink in the bar, and any initial resentment at having to babysit a training exercise was nothing but a memory by the second week. The group was a tight one, but they never failed to welcome a new face; even Hieron was starting to come out of his shell, for which he would always thank Fleck. It was not home, not by a long way; but it was comfortable, and he counted the people his friends.

Eventually, however, the training was over and they made the long trip back to Alamo Station. The knowledge that they would not necessarily meet each other again prompted many promises of long-range correspondence, and a pledge to come together for a drink after Tortuga to celebrate their victory. The fact that victory was far from assured, or that they knew many of their group would likely not be returning, was never mentioned; they all knew it, and there was no point dwelling on what they could do nothing about.

The pilots were each to be assigned a training group of one hundred, so that their new expertise could be passed on to as many as possible. With luck, and training, they would have over four hundred pilots ready to face the array in ships that were far more manoeuvrable than before, both in terms of the ship's own design, and the greatly reduced reaction time afforded by the EEG chips.

The rest of the training was not foremost in Hieron's mind, however, as they finally arrived aboard Alamo Station. He tolerantly sat through the debriefing, his mind trying to wander off throughout; then he walked swiftly to his quarters where his wife would be waiting for him. He opened the door and stepped through, eagerly calling to her as he did so. But she was nowhere to be found. Perhaps they had switched her shifts around, he thought. But no, she would have demanded to be on down time when her husband's ship put in.

He went to the hangar to look for her - maybe she had tried to meet him there and they had missed each other in the crowd. Along the way, he ran into Kiah coming the opposite direction; the white-haired man's face became somber upon meeting Hieron, and he stopped the pilot to talk. "Hieron," he began, clasping his friend's hand in greeting. "Welcome back my friend, it is truly a balm to my spirit to see you once more. I only wish I had better news to give to you. Perhaps this would be best communicated in my office."

Hieron's mind raced as he followed the acolyte the short distance to his office; it had to be about Klaira - but what? Had she disappeared? Been injured in an industrial accident? Had she lost the baby? He was going to blurt all of these things out at Kiah when they arrived, but the acolyte stopped him. "Listen to me," he told him.

"Your wife experienced complications in her pregnancy, and I sent her to Earth to receive specialist treatment. Unfortunately, the shuttle experienced a catastrophic drive failure while in hyperspace, and was lost with all hands. I am so sorry Hieron, it was my fault."

Hieron sat, numb and terribly alone as the world shrank away from him. He remembered little of the next few days, spent as they were in a haze of tears, drinking, and gazing unfeelingly into space. His first clear memory after talking with Kiah was meeting the acolyte again to tell him that it was not his fault, and that he did the right thing. They embraced as friends, and the relief in Kiah's eyes was easy to see; Hieron had tried to blame him but had failed. His mind was simply too rational to accept that Kiah had done anything he himself would not have done in his place. In fact, his recovery from this fresh trauma surprised everyone who knew him, and they began to suspect that he was keeping something from them. Fleck visited him on the night before he was due to ship out for the next round of training, trying to ascertain whether he was truly ready and fit for command. He assured her he was.

"Sure, you're just fine," she mocked. "It's not like your wife and child were just ripped out of your life as if they'd never been there." That earned her a baleful glare from her friend.

"I am not fine, Vesta," he growled. "But I am fit to lead this training, so go tell the Council you did your job and I can go do mine."

"You think the Council sent me?" she asked quietly. "You think the only reason I'm here is to rubber stamp some form to tell everyone you're fit for command?" He shrugged, defiant of the offence she was clearly taking. "You know what, Hieron Tomac? Fuck you." Tears were in her eyes as she left him sat alone on his bunk, and he quietly cursed to himself.

# Part Four
## Chapter 13

The probe was as small as it could be while still containing a rudimentary hyperspace drive and communications array. Due to the nature of hyperspace travel, this meant that it could shoot from one system to another in mere seconds, relaying messages in very nearly real-time - another technology advance that had vastly improved response time for reinforcement fleets. Hieron was eating his lunch in the refectory aboard the *Firebird* when the message reached them from the probe. It had been sent by Admiral Fleck from the *Concord*, and was a request for all available Navy personnel to converge on the Tortuga system. What was missing, however, was the code attached to the message to signify that it was yet another of the endless drills they had been running for the past two months. This was the real thing. The array had reentered human space at Tortuga, precisely on schedule and on target.

Hieron had been given command of a relatively small fleet which was stationed in the Ulysses system, one short jump from Tortuga, for the eventuality that the array struck there instead. No chances were being taken, but it meant that the fleet was not concentrated at the most likely point of attack, and they had approximately thirty minutes to get to safe distance from the planet's gravity well and make - and complete - the jump to hyperspace. Their average time on the drills lately had been thirty six.

Hieron's fleet was tiny by comparison to the rest of the forces Unity had gathered in Tortuga, consisting as it did of five Valkyries, two of which carried eight Polecats between them, the other three carrying eighteen Lightnings. Yet when he compared it to the first sortie he had led against the pirates of Juliano station a lifetime ago, it seemed overwhelmingly strong. The array was stronger, though; he knew that much. They would need all their gathered might to resist its seemingly inexorable advance. He only hoped that they would not need more.

The pilots all scrambled to their fighters as the Valkyries manoeuvred to their designated jump coordinates; it had been decided that, though the fighters could make the jump in significantly less time than the larger cruisers, they would opt to carry them instead, in order to make a single, unified assault force. It would do little good if the Valkyries arrived to find their fighters already destroyed by the array. They would launch immediately upon arrival, however, and had to be prepared for it.

Hieron lowered himself into the comfortably familiar surroundings of the cockpit and initialised the virtual link between his chip and the computer system. He immediately got a sense of the status of the craft, and knew that everything was fine; the chip seemed to communicate mostly through feelings such as unease, so if there was a problem with the fuel systems he would immediately become worried about them. It was not the most ideal set up, but it was apparently the best they had found so far. He continued to manually check over the system readouts, to be absolutely certain that nothing was about to fall off as soon as he launched; after a few minutes he received the notification that the fleet was jumping to hyperspace. The journey would take twenty nine minutes and forty two seconds, as it always did; by his calculations they would arrive thirty three minutes after having received the summons.

It was the longest twenty nine minutes and forty two seconds of his life; he lost count of how many times he checked and rechecked the instruments, rehearsed strategies and manoeuvres in his head, and eventually started counting bulkhead panels. He had counted them all five times when the signal came that they were thirty seconds from exiting hyperspace. The docking clamps were released, and he looked right to see Arno sat in his Polecat a dozen yards away, who caught his glance and gave him a thumbs-up. The kid was still yet to see any real action - certainly the minor skirmishes he had experienced had involved no Unity losses at all. Hieron hoped he would be able to cope with the reality of losing friends in an instant. He reciprocated the gesture, though, and returned his gaze to the launch rail in front of him. Across his fleet, twenty five other pilots were sharing the same view, with likely the same thoughts; was this to be their end, or perhaps even the beginning of the end of humanity itself? Thoughts inevitably focused on those left behind - friends, family, comrades, even enemies.

Hieron's thoughts were darker than most, however. Though he too thought of those left behind, his chief thought was for his wife and son, for whom he was the one left behind. Far better, he thought, to be the one leaving than the one left. He activated the engines on cue as the Valkyrie exited hyperspace and the fighter bay was automatically depressurised, watching the huge doors slide away revealing the pinpricked blackness beyond. The brakes were straining against the thrust of the engines, and he released them, signalling the other fighters to do the same. He and Arno were hurled down the launch rail and out into the black within a second, and wheeled about to form up together in support of the cruisers.

Ahead of them was a scene from his nightmares. The array was as immense as he had remembered it, dwarfing the eight huge Mastodons arrayed against it, and had already begun to separate into the flower-like shape as it launched a cloud of the tiny laser drones to harass the Unity fleet. Hieron's own ships wasted no time in powering forward at the greatest velocity the Valkyries could manage, closing the gap slowly but surely. Communications flashed back and forth between the different elements of the fleet, and Hieron had never heard a comm channel so packed with voices. It was a blessing the individual fighter pilots' voices were not thrown into the mix, or it simply would have been impossible to send or receive any orders at all.

A minute passed before the first long-range munitions started to be launched by the Valkyries, torpedoes with a large payload and range but minimal guidance. They drifted gracefully across the black and were swallowed by it; the scanner showed them continue on target, and by the time they impacted upon the core of the - now fully deployed - array, the fighters were in range. A wall of missiles was released and shot forward at many times the speed of the torpedoes. The space above the planet was a writhing mass of ships, ordnance, and laser fire; the closer they drew to the thick of the fight, the messier it looked. He willed his ship to go faster, and it shot away from the formation like a bullet; he had stopped caring about hitting them hard and all at once. It was not going to make a difference when they got there.

125

The megacannons mounted on the six orbital platforms were firing shot after shot into the hub of the array, with no apparent effect; glancing out at the closest, Hieron watched as a group of the tiny alien drones quickly and efficiently cut the cannon from its mounting as if they were performing an amputation. Powerless, it floated free to join the growing debris field in orbit around Tortuga. Hieron knew it would not be long before the other cannons met the same fate. A few seconds from the edges of the battle, he concentrated on the voices chattering back and forth across the comm channel, ignoring the calls from his own fleet about his breaking formation. Damage reports comprised the majority of the chatter, and it seemed that one of the Mastodons had been completely gutted by the drones. Assessments of the damage done to the array itself were more vague and even less encouraging; it was showing no signs of distress whatsoever, the munitions exploding against its core seeming to make no difference.

An idea struck him, but he soon lost the thread of it as a drone closed in on him and he tumbled into the mêlée. From the chatter, he picked up his first bit of good news; it seemed that the drones lacked whatever heavy armour or shielding it was that afforded the array's hub its seeming invulnerability. They weren't falling easily to the human weapons, but they were falling. Hieron's Polecat ducked and wove through the enormous dogfight, banking to port and to starboard as the drone's laser tried to cut through his shields. He wheeled about in a tight arc and managed to get a few good shots in on the alien weapon before having to evade once again. Passing fighters took their own shots at his drone, and he returned the favour a number of times. Finally, a missile out of nowhere struck it full on the stern and ended its pursuit. He never discovered who had fired the missile, but it hardly mattered - lives were being saved in every corner of the battle, and the favours were not being tallied.

The rest of Hieron's fleet had merged with the main bulk of the Unity force, thereby committing the very last ships that humanity could spare in its defence. Over a third of the fighters they had brought to the battle had already been lost, but they were the unskilled and the unlucky; the losses would slow now that the weak had been cut from the ranks. As Hieron caught the rhythm of the fight, he allowed himself to focus on the manoeuvres with slightly less than his full concentration, so as to try to recapture that elusive thought. It had begun when anticipating the first of the drones, and the cutting lasers that they wielded with thoughtless accuracy. It was something about their shape, somewhat resembling an arrow from ancient warfare; it was tantalising to recall the feeling that a desperately important answer was so close, and yet just out of reach.

- - - - -

Admiral Fleck was not enjoying herself even a little bit. If it wasn't enough that the array was showing no signs at all of weakening under their heaviest assaults, she was also getting reports that Hieron's fleet arrived in disorder, their leader pulling away from the formation prior to contact with the enemy. It was not so much the breach of protocol or orders she was concerned about, but that she was going to lose her friend to the demons in his own head. She had been watching him in the weeks leading up to the battle, even though she had not spoken to him since telling him in no uncertain terms what she thought of his facade of normality. He had seemed fine, and even she began to doubt her assessment of his condition - until she had overheard a conversation between Kiah and Hieron outside the Council conference room.

"I don't care about your Grand Destiny," Hieron had stated with his voice raised defiantly. "If it's all set in stone then nothing I can do will change it anyway, right?"

"That's not exactly how it works, my friend," Kiah had assured him in his usual, calm tone. "There are subtle nuances to Fate that are difficult to fathom; your destiny is set, so it is the resistance itself that is pointless."

"I am not an asset, Kiah," Hieron had growled. "I am not a commodity that you need to protect. What I am is one of the best damn pilots in all of Unity, and it makes no sense to have me stationed anywhere other than the front line!"

"The array is not necessarily as predictable as we think, Hieron. What if it reaches Tortuga and deploys a completely new weapon, incinerating everyone and everything there in an instant? Then where will we be but stranded, without 'the best pilot in all of Unity'?"

"I need to be there, Kiah," Hieron had lowered his voice, speaking seriously with a suggestion of desperation in his tone.

"You will be there, my friend," Kiah had reassured him. "Believe me, you'll be there. But not on the front line; you'll be heading up the task force from Ulysses as discussed. There is nothing more to be said." The men had parted ways, and Vesta had thought long about why Hieron might be so insistent on being stationed at Tortuga when the array reappeared. She hoped it was a simple case of revenge, of purging the demons of Korpi once and for all; but part of her suspected that it was something more. The man had lost his wife and child and shown little if any outward signs of emotion after the first few days. Vesta had heard of pilots in similar situations before, who had seemed perfectly fine until their next battle, when they had become reckless and fought only to die.

So it was with a terrible sinking feeling that she received the news of his precipitous advance, knowing what it might signify for her old friend and comrade. There was so little she could do from the command deck of the Concord, though, and she felt powerless; it was times like this that she envied the faith that most of the rest of her crew - and the Navy as a whole - shared. Irrational though she knew it was, it clearly offered comfort when one felt powerless against what might be considered Fate. Cursing the idea of destiny, and Hieron's recklessness, she contacted the wing of Polecats that had launched from the Concord less than an hour ago, and told them to protect Hieron's own Polecat as best they could. He was going to survive this battle whether he wanted to or not, if she had anything to do with it.

The third orbital platform had been completely disabled, as the fourth megacannon was cut from its hull rendering it defenceless. As much as it was a galling setback for Unity, she saw it as a positive sign - the drones would not be attempting to remove the cannons if they did not pose a significant threat to the array itself. As comforting as that thought was, however, it was balanced by the knowledge that the cannons were nevertheless being destroyed at a prodigious rate, and the array seemed entirely unaffected by their onslaught. Perhaps, she thought suddenly, the cannons were not a current threat, but a potential one; it was possible that they were simply not being used to greatest effect.

"Contact Commander Jenito," she ordered her comm officer. "Tell him to reassign targets for the remaining platform cannons. Target the array's support struts and resume fire at will." The order was relayed and she waited as the heavy shots from the megacannons fell silent. If her hunch was right, then they were about to experience a change of fortunes. She watched the view screen as the destructive ballet went on about them, trying not to think of the lives lost every time a Unity fighter was destroyed. It had to be worth it. Every second bought at the cost of a life was one more second they had to destroy the array.

The cannons opened fire again, and the targeting computers were put to their most trying test yet as they attempted to hit a span of something - that was presumably metal - measuring less than a metre in diameter. Considering this, and the range at which they were operating, they did admirably well, with only two shots of every five falling wide of the mark. The damage done was not as dramatic as she would have liked, but scorch marks soon became visible on the copper surface. If they could only keep up the assault, she felt sure that the struts could be severed; though what might happen then was anybody's guess.

The drones were too numerous and too efficient, however; the cannons managed perhaps five minutes of barrage upon the superstructure of the array before they were permanently silenced. She gazed in despondent resignation as the last of the cannons floated harmlessly into the orbit of Tortuga, and for the first time started to truly doubt that humanity could halt the advance of the array into their space. Reports from sensors deployed on the surface of the planet indicated that the temperature already exceeded the maximum safe level for human habitation, and it would not be long before it was just another ball of ash like Korpi. She was snapped from her reverie by a familiar voice coming over the comm system.

"Tomac to Fleck. Admiral, has your science officer managed to make a chemical analysis of the drones yet?" She glanced at the scanner and wondered how he was able to let his mind wander while dancing with death out in the thick of the heaviest fighting.

"I think so," she responded. "I'll put the report through to you now."

"Not the best of times," he replied, merely a slight note of tension in his voice. "I sort of have my hands full at the moment, you might have noticed. Just tell me if these little *fuckers* are magnetic." It rare for Hieron to swear, and Fleck interpreted that to mean that he was finding the going far more rough than his voice was letting on. She shot a meaningful interrogative look at her science officer, and the woman nodded, hands flying over the instrument panel before her. A few moments later she turned back to the Admiral and nodded again.

"It seems they contain significant enough amounts of iron to make them magnetic, Tomac," She relayed to the pilot. "What are you thinking?"

"I'll let you know when it works," came the terse and enigmatic response.

- - - - -

"All right you son of a bitch," Hieron muttered at the drone he had been alternately chasing and evading for the past several minutes. "Let's see exactly how fast you really are." *And how fast this 'cat is*, he added in his head as he tossed the ship into a series of banks and turns that exceeded anything he had managed before. He was not trying to destroy the drone this time, and had made sure to warn off his wingmen from doing the job for him. He had noticed that the drones had a small range of manoeuvres in their repertoire, whether that was due to limited programming of their guidance systems or a lack of imagination on the part of the hypothetically-plausible pilot. Whatever the cause, the longer he jousted with them, the more predictable he found their movements to be; if he pulled in behind it like *this*, it would dive; if he followed, it would reverse its dive and start to climb again. But if he had been holding back on the throttle, then there was a window at that point where he could shoot forward and be directly on top of the drone.

The scanner showed their blips converging and he watched closely as they seemed to merge. Then he activated the magnetic landing brake on the belly of the Polecat, and felt a satisfying jolt as the drone was attached to his underside. The laser beam lanced into the space before his bow in a constant line, and he did not stop to wonder why that might have happened; there would be time for that later. For the time being, he flew swiftly toward the array, careful not to touch the laser beam to any Unity craft. It was not at all easy in the mêlée, and twice he scored the shield of a friendly fighter as they passed before him.

Finally he reached the array, immense and mysterious, and slowed his craft. Then, with a series of carefully-aimed runs, he focused the drone's beam weapon upon the array's support struts, cutting through the copper-coloured span as easily as a knife through flesh. Before long, one of the petal-like arms of the array was floating free to join the megacannons and ship debris floating in the orbit of Tortuga. He immediately relayed his idea to Vesta aboard the *Concord*, and continued the work; before long, he was joined by Arno with his own attached drone, and eventually three more pilots skilled enough to capture alien drones of their own. Together they dissected the array, removing limb after limb until nothing remained but the central hub, huge and unmarked by the earlier onslaught.

Just as their elation at the change in fortunes was beginning to wear off, the array turned from the planet with ominous slowness. Thinking it may have been attempting to retreat, the fighters made several runs against it, scoring their laser beams across its glossy, golden surface. Unlike the shots from the megacannon, these weapons did leave a blackened trace behind them, but little damage was otherwise apparent as the array turned. When it was facing the closest of the five Mastodons now remaining, its central assembly began to glow a deep red; Hieron guessed what was happening and attempted to contact the capital ship to relay a warning to them, but it was already too late. The Mastodon began to glow in a grim facsimile of the array, and the imagined screams of the dying as they were roasted alive sprang unbidden back into Hieron's mind. He tried not to think of the exact number of crew serving aboard the ship, as its fuel reserves reached their flash point and ignited, feeding hungrily on the remaining oxygen in the interior of the ship.

The array swivelled again, coming about to face the next capital ship and focusing its devastating weapon upon it. A Polecat making a run against the array was unfortunate enough to be caught in the crossfire and was incinerated in the blink of an eye. Hieron ordered the remaining three pilots to focus their assault runs against the central weapon assembly on the array, but also to stay well clear of the weapon itself. It was only when he heard their various voices in acknowledgment of his order when he realised that the pilot who had just been destroyed was Arno, the wide-eyed and gifted recruit he had met on the *Firebird*. He pushed down the anguish to be dealt with later, but kept a portion of the anger present at the front of his mind. It would be useful in the next few critical minutes.

The black lines on the array's surface were widening, and if his eyes were not deceiving him, deepening also. They kept up their formation assault as the second Mastodon erupted a short distance away, each of them vowing their vengeance in the silent privacy of their cockpits. They kept their distance as the array turned once again to focus its terrible attention upon the next Unity capital ship, which was attempting to take evasive action - though its engines were not powerful enough to move it very fast. Glancing up, Hieron saw he was close enough to make out the markings on the Mastodon's hull, and immediately wished he was not. It was the *Concord*.

- - - - -

"Keep that fucking beam off us!" Vesta shouted, having already exhausted the small range of specific orders at her disposal. Extra power was being diverted from the shields to the engines, risking the attacks of the drones for the possibility of evading the main array. The smaller ships were making a point of avoiding the space to the stern of the *Concord*, knowing what would happen to them if they strayed within the targeting area of the alien weapon. Even the majority, who believed strongly in an idyllic afterlife, had no wish to join it just yet.

As the *Concord* ploughed through the battle, fighters scattered left and right as they tried to evade their drones and avoid a collision with the capital ship at the same time. Then Vesta saw the other Mastodon, the *UNS Synthesis*, crossing their path to the port stern; before she had a chance to call a warning, the array had ceased tracking the *Concord* and focused its attention on the *Synthesis*, already heavily damaged and unable to spare any additional power to its engines. It did not take long for the weapon to be brought to bear upon the broken craft, and the sickeningly familiar glow began once again across its scarred hull. She willed them to launch the escape pods and abandon their ship to its fate, and then had to look away as her wish was granted too late. Dozens of escape pods burst from the redly glowing flank of the *Synthesis*, each and every one detonating immediately. It was like some horrific firework display and made Vesta feel sick to her stomach.

"Maintain speed," she ordered through gritted teeth. "Bring us about to an intercept course with that bastard thing." Her order was acknowledged, and she noted the confusion and concern in the faces of her command crew. But a good commander did not explain her orders, and a good crew followed them no matter what their own personal feelings were on the matter. The Mastodon swung about as the array attempted to acquire its next target. A dozen drones broke off their attack on the fighters and swarmed toward the capital ship, laser beams cutting mercilessly into the vessel's weakened shield. She called for fighter support but the drones were too quick and too determined to see the *Concord* destroyed.

Shields failed, and the lasers began to cut through the hull, severing power to the weapons and life support. There was nothing else for it. She opened a comm channel to the rest of the ship. "Attention all hands. This is Admiral Fleck. Weapons and life support are offline, we're on a sinking ship. All hands are to report to the escape pod decks immediately and set course for the orbit of the second planet in the system. Abandon ship. Repeat, abandon ship." The bridge crew looked at her as one. "That goes for you too, you know. I did say 'all hands' didn't I? Fairly sure that's what I said." They stood, saluted, and left. They knew what she was planning, and she did not blame them for opting out; if any of them had tried to stay, she would have stuffed them into the escape pods herself.

The display in front of her notified her of the status of the launch, and within just two short minutes she was officially alone aboard the immense Mastodon, rapidly losing power and air as the drones continued to cut chunks from her structure. She keyed the main view screen to display what was directly in front of the ship, with no magnification; she could just make out the array in the distance, a maliciously glinting red eye against the black nothing of space. It was turning to cast its deadly gaze directly upon her, she knew. But it was slow, and she was fast; and momentum was a wonderful thing.

- - - - -

Hieron was starting to wonder how long it would take to cut deep enough to cause permanent damage to the array; they had been at it for what seemed forever, back and forth in a practiced rhythm. The cuts were getting deeper, certainly; but the weapon was still active, and pointed almost straight at his friend's vessel. Just as he thought they would never succeed, however, the energy readings from the weapon began to fall gradually, and the glow from its center began to subside.

The array continued turning, however, and the glow at its centre was still menacingly strong. Hieron glanced at his scanner, and saw the *Concord* on a direct collision course with the array, closing fast; he looked out to starboard and saw her, careening in faster than she should have been able to manage. The bow was starting to glow red as she approached, and he tried to contact Vesta to tell her to break off her run and evade; that the array's weapon was no longer a threat.  His warnings were met with static, which meant there was nobody on board, or they were ignoring him, or their communications systems were down.  He was not sure which he would wish for more, but wasted no time in telling the other Polecats to scatter.  Whatever happened in the next few seconds, there was going to be an almighty explosion and that sort of kinetic force could take a fighter apart all by itself.

The *Concord*'s bow was glowing brightly now, as the depleting energy of the array's weapon seared into it.  The two points of red light converged and met, the Unity ship's momentum carrying it full into the face of the weapon.  For a moment it seemed that the two objects merged as if one were absorbing the other; but then there was an almighty detonation that sent Hieron and the other fleeing Polecats spinning out of control.  In the same instant, the laser drones on their bellies appeared to cease functioning, the continuous beams cutting out for the first time since their capture.  The scanner showed no sign of the array, nor any of the Mastodon; Unity ships were scattered like leaves on the wind, but there were no more aliens to threaten them. They had survived, and they had won.

# Chapter 14

The mass funeral for all those lost at Tortuga was held a month later in the main hangar of Alamo Station. The survivors - just two hundred of them out of a force of over one thousand - took pride of place at the forefront of the assembly, their copper-coloured Tortuga medals gleaming in a strange echo of the array itself. Kiah had talked Hieron into making the main speech, and his heart was heavy with both grief and dread as he anticipated the moment he would take the platform. The list was being read of all the names of those lost in the battle, beginning with the lowest ranks and culminating in his friend, Admiral Vesta Fleck; tears welled and he tried to push them down, knowing it was almost time for him to speak. He failed, and as the speaker introduced him, and the Unity News cameras swivelled onto him, the tears were flowing freely down his face. He stood anyway, and dabbed a hand at his eyes as he walked to the podium.

"We are here today to remember all those who have just been named," he began, voice shaking slightly. "Their sacrifice has ensured the survival of humanity as a species, and should never be underestimated. The Battle of Tortuga was the culmination of ten years of careful planning, of necessarily strict rules and tightened belts. But just because it is over, and the array is destroyed, does not mean that we must give up what great good has come of it. Humanity is united for the first time since we stepped out of our home system and made a bid for the stars beyond; why should we give that up now that the threat that united us is passed? To do so would be recklessness of the highest order, and more than that it would dishonour the sacrifice of those who bought our freedom with their lives - in the name of Unity.

"So as we gather to honour the fallen, and remember their sacrifice, let us not throw away the co-operation and the freedom for which they fought so hard. Let us all come together today in mourning for those we have lost, and in celebration of what we have achieved together with their help. We must remain strong for their sake, for we do not know whether there will one day be another alien array striking at humanity without cause or warning. For the sake of those who have fallen in defence of Unity, we must remain united."

It was hardly the most elegant speech, but he had not had the will to prepare properly. Looking about as he descended to the floor again, he saw Kiah's smile and knew it must have been at least adequate. The white-haired man had impressed upon him the need to reiterate the necessity of Unity in the wake of the end of what had sparked its creation. Unity would remain as the sole governing body of humanity in the galaxy, not just because of the threat of future alien incursions, but because it worked. While there was still great inequality between the core worlds and the outlier colonies, nobody was starving, and no area wanted for sufficient law enforcement.

The Navy would remain strong, rebuilding from its losses at Tortuga and fortifying the Galactic South West with outposts and sensor buoys, to avoid being taken by surprise once more. Rebellions continued to spring up, and with renewed vigour now that what many saw as the only reason for remaining united had passed. They were quashed as quickly as they began, sometimes simply by the correct application of a unit of Predators, and sometimes by the full force of the Unity Navy. Sanctions were introduced against some of the outlier systems that caused perennial unrest, and missionaries from the Church of Intentionality increased the frequency of their visits and the vigour of their sermons on cooperation and destiny.

Hieron, meanwhile, was under a different kind of pressure altogether. Somehow he had been awarded the epithet 'Hero of Tortuga' for his idea with the magnetic docking brakes, and no matter how hard he insisted that the woman flying the *Concord* into the hub of the array was the real hero, the name stuck. After every session of the Council, Kiah would approach him privately and appeal to Hieron to speak up more and take a stand against the continuous squabbling of the stuffed shirts within. There were certainly a great number of policies with which Hieron did not agree, he admitted to himself, but he simply did not think of himself as a politician, let alone a suitable leader.

His dreams, too, became more troubled; he realised how much of a distraction the impending battle had been, with so many decisions and preparations to make. He had not had the time to worry, or to remember Klaira and his son. Now that his worries were reduced to relative trivialities, everything he had pushed to the back of his mind was mounting a counterattack on his conscious mind. Most troubling of all were the dreams in which his wife appeared to him aboard the shuttle on which she had been killed, pleading with him to save her. She would invariably blame the situation on imbalance, which infuriated him even more in the dream than it had in reality. He tried to argue but found he did not believe his own words. The other dreams, horrific though they often were, did not leave him any more troubled in the waking world; it was only this one that made him doubt whether he was doing the right thing.

- - - - -

Try as he might, Kiah was having difficulty keeping Hieron on track. The man seemed to have no ambition, no drive whatsoever to be better than he was; Kiah was certain this was just because of the losses he had suffered and his need to grieve, but it was becoming frustrating. Their latest meeting actually involved the 'hero of Tortuga' questioning the necessity of their various vital revenue projects in the outlier systems; that kind of nonsense had to be headed off immediately before it got any worse. Kiah had just the solution: if Hieron was unwilling to step forward to take the position that called out to him, then he would simply have to have greatness thrust upon him.

So it was that he sat with amused patience through the next session of the Unity Council, enduring the petty bureaucrats attempting to exercise what little power was accorded to them, and butting up against each other in the process. It was ironic, he thought, that Unity was ruled by such discord; but that contradiction would not last much longer. They were so wrapped up in their wrangling that they seemed to entirely miss the fact that Hieron himself was absent.

The topic of the discussion on that day was one in which he had great interest: the efficacy of the Church campaign for peace and unity. Yet still the talk around the table both bored and frustrated him. The representatives of the Earth States Commonwealth were the most vocal by far, and yet the ones with least knowledge of the galaxy, and least stake in the outcome as Earth was almost completely peaceful. It was because they were elected with at least the illusion of democracy, Kiah decided. This thin veneer of representative accountability gave these petty, ignorant politicians an excuse to be outspoken on every issue, to claim to be an expert no matter how complex the topic discussed. Because if they did not make their voices heard, then perhaps the masses would elect somebody louder and more outspoken to be their representative on the Council.

This is what democracy led to, Kiah saw. Either the people elected who they really wanted to lead them - and that person turned out to be incompetent, corrupt, or simply not up to the job - or the broken system spat out another loud-mouthed, ignorant bully who thought she was far more important than she actually was. It was a system which was no longer useful to humanity, if indeed it ever had been. But that would be dealt with all in good time; and the first step would be taken today. His idle mind drifted back into the conversation, and he was unsurprised to hear Mentero, the Mexican representative for North America, speaking pompously of the need for more Church officials to visit his constituents.

"It is simply a matter of necessity," he asserted. "My region -"

"Has one of the highest Church attendance rates in the entire galaxy," the Australasian representative finished for him. "You can't argue that you need more missionaries on that - or any - basis. In fact," she continued, beginning what they all knew was coming, "I have yet to see any convincing figures that the Church officials are doing any good whatsoever - except toward lining the Church's pockets with donations of the faithful." The Council's reaction was interesting, Kiah noted; a few looked outraged, a few seemed to be embarrassed by her inevitable contrariness, and the rest smiled derisively. It was not surprising that Australasia had elected a non-spiritualist to the Council, being the area with the least faith in the Great Destiny overall, but what was surprising was that she remained so outspokenly non-spiritual within the Council sessions. Peer pressure was a powerful force, and one that the Church exploited regularly. Yet, it seemed, she was unaffected by the varying expressions of disapproval around the table, continuing to wax lyrical about the figures surrounding the efficacy of the Church in maintaining peace.

Finally, when her speech ran out of steam, the rest of the Council resumed their discussion as if she had never spoken, and she sat back in her chair with a scowl on her face. Kiah continued to observe the proceedings passively, despite his significant stake in their outcome. Truth be told, he was not a little fascinated by the human compulsion to continually contradict one's political rivals even when the points being discussed were areas of broad agreement between the parties. It was hardly conducive to unity and harmony, but that did not stop it from being rather interesting. Alliances between the Council members formed and were discarded without ever being discussed, and new rivalries and enmities were born regularly. Every slight, actual or imagined, was mentally filed away and its exact degree of offence calculated for the purposes of future reprisal.

This is what people wanted from their governments, Kiah realised; they might desire strong leadership and a unified policy, but what they really wanted to see was the raw flesh of the political process. They wanted to see that their policies came out of a no-holds-barred, violent debate. He was not even sure that the outcome would be important to them, if only they could see that the government cared enough about the issues to argue about them. He would have to bear that in mind. Perhaps it would make sense to have a televised debate every so often, or just film a session of the Council. As long as they discussed nothing that it was not appropriate for the public to hear, it could be just the thing to stop them wondering about the secretive meetings of the Council.

His attention drifted back to the ongoing discussion, just as Langton Parnett spoke up. Partly due to the depth of his rumbling baritone, and partly to the rarity of his speaking, an unusual hush had fallen across the other members of the Council. The tall man seemed not to notice, but Kiah knew he missed nothing. "From what I can see," he began, "this group could itself use a little more unity. What kind of example are we setting by jumping down each others' throats like this, day after day? It's better than solving our problems with guns, yes, but is it truly that far removed?" Kiah wondered, for an entirely irrational moment, if the CEO of Arbiter Fuels was some kind of mind reader. Whether he was or not, the acolyte leapt upon the opportunity like a cat on a mouse.

"Well said, Mr Parnett," he announced with a suddenness that made several Council members jolt. "Unity led by disunity is a contradiction, and one that must be rectified. What we need is one figure to unite all policy, with enough power to overrule any Council decision that is deemed to not be in the best interests of humanity as a whole. No more alliances, no more back-handers, no more backstabbing - any self interest will be effectively filtered out by the addition of a supreme position placed above the Council itself." He did not have to be a mind reader himself to know what the majority of them were expecting: that he himself would be the one to lead them in this manner. So he savoured the blank surprise upon their faces when he announced his true intention. "I move for this Council to appoint Commander Hieron Tomac to the new position of Archon, with supreme executive power over the decisions of the Council and the ultimate actions of Unity. A simple majority vote will suffice," he added.

The silence was total, each member of the Council looking to the others, perhaps trying to reassure themselves that it was actually happening. Most of them had guessed or discovered that Kiah had plans to create such a position, but they had assumed he would suggest himself, and had prepared their responses accordingly. Now that they had to consider a different man for the job, it changed things enough that they were no longer certain that they would object to the situation. He hurried them by asking for all in favour to show their hands. Kiah raised his own, and was joined by General Leetman. Shortly, two more hands went up, the owners of those hands perhaps relieved that it would be someone other than the acolyte, or perhaps simply looking for an end to the cutthroat politics of the Council's daily life. It was an appealing proposition, and another hand raised. It belonged to the Australasian representative; Kiah had been careful to drop some hints recently suggesting that Hieron's faith in the Great Destiny was shaky at best, which had effectively secured the outspoken woman's vote.

He surveyed the room, counting the votes and calculating his next move. He needed eight votes, or at least he needed for the dissenters to number fewer than eight; a majority of those voting would suffice, so abstainers counted for neither side. He currently had five hands in the air. It was too early to risk checking the numbers on the other side; if nobody abstained, he would be sunk. He tried to gauge the mood of the Council, something at which he was becoming more adept by the day. Parnett was playing his hand close to his chest, as usual, and Kiah had little hope of guessing what he would do until it was done; he could probably count on the votes of the other half of the corporate heads - he knew they were most of them tired of the heavy-handed politics that the ESC representatives had brought with them, and were keen to stop playing a game for which they had not signed up. Those that did not vote for him would most likely abstain. Another hand went up, this one belonging to Wareck Gendson; Kiah hid his surprise and excitement. Gendson hated Hieron, but apparently he hated the Earth reps more, and this meant that Kiah needed just four people to abstain.

He took the chance, and asked for all against. Immediately the six raised hands dropped, and were replaced by six others, and Kiah's heart leapt to his throat; it was too close. Three abstentions, including Parnett, were experiencing the most power they would ever hold; the Asian representative seemed to be enjoying it, and Ari Zack seemed to be feeling even more uncomfortable than usual at the prospect. Parnett remained inevitably impassive. Considering the fervour with which the six 'against' votes had been cast, Kiah knew there would be no swaying their decisions. It now all rested upon the abstainers. The Earth rep would probably vote with the majority of the others if pushed, and Kiah was fairly certain he could intimidate Zack into voting in favour; that left Langton Parnett as possibly the most powerful man in the galaxy at that very moment.

Sure enough it took only a brief discussion for the dissenters to secure the Asian representative's vote in their camp, and this was shortly followed by the crumbling of what resolve the Tranquility Shipyards' CEO had remaining. All eyes turned to Parnett, the head of Arbiter Fuels and Hieron's former employer. He had made no secret of his opposition to many of the Council's policies over recent years, but which way this might swing his vote was entirely unpredictable. The pessimists on each side of the vote saw him joining the other, either to scupper another of Kiah's plans, or to remain loyal to Hieron. Kiah appealed to him to settle the deadlock, and reminded him that abstentions were not permitted in such a situation.

"I am aware of the rules, Master Sicarius," he reminded the impatient white-haired man. "I did help to write them, after all." He ran a hand through his short, greying hair; to think he had been a relatively young man when this all started. "I believe Hieron is a wise man," he said finally, each person gathered around the table hanging on every implication in his words and the tone in which they were delivered. "I think you know I care little for politics, or rather the petty backstabbing that the word so often implies. I have always tailored my vote to what I believe to be the best interests of humanity. The Great Destiny is a mystery to me, as it is to all but the wisest of men." He glanced at Kiah, either as a tribute to his wisdom, or to suggest that that wisdom was significantly lacking. "I know Hieron better than most," he continued, "and his is a troubled soul. His past is a rocky one, and recent years have done nothing to heal old wounds, losing as he has not only his wife, but his unborn son and closest friend - to say nothing of the massacre he had to witness at Korpi.

"After that first encounter with the array, and the trauma of losing so many placed in his care, we all doubted whether he would be capable of leading our combined forces again. We must surely be asking ourselves the same questions now, and perhaps that is why some of you have voted against the motion. I myself have never doubted his ability to lead, and indeed to act in the best interests of the species as a whole; but my own doubts are of a personal nature. I have recently wondered if it is not terribly cruel to be heaping so much responsibility upon those troubled shoulders, and whether the most compassionate course would be to relieve him of all his worries and allow him the leisure to address them in his own time."

The dissenters were beginning to look victorious as they saw where they assumed Parnett's uncharacteristically verbose speech to be heading. The European representative even went so far as to propose a financial plan to support Hieron in his early retirement and help him to get the counselling he clearly needed. Parnett smiled a thin smile. "Your concern is an inspiration to us all, and a reminder to keep compassion at the forefront of our endeavours," he rumbled back. "However, I believe it may be somewhat premature. I spoke to Hieron privately just a few days ago, and while my opinion is far from that of a professional, as a friend I can clearly see that time off is not what he needs. He needs something to throw himself into, a project to keep his mind occupied as it was in the run-up to Tortuga. And, as I mentioned, he is a wise man. If we are to have a supreme leader in control of this assembly, I can think of few people better suited to the role - and few roles better suited to my friend Mr Tomac."

Kiah could hardly contain himself. "So your vote is in favour of the motion?" he asked, suppressing his eagerness as best as he possibly could. Parnett nodded, and the release of emotion could be heard in various noises around the room. Kiah himself felt like singing, and dissolved the meeting to go and give Hieron the news; he would never forgive himself if somebody managed to tell Hieron before he had the chance. The Council agreed to meet again the next day to formalise the new arrangements and Kiah rushed off down the corridor.

- - - - -

Hieron was not in the mood for foolery when Kiah entered, breathless and gabbling something about a momentous turn of events. He had never seen the acolyte so animated, and it was almost like seeing an excited child who was trying to explain the reason for their excitement to an infuriatingly obtuse adult who seemed unable to understand communication through gasps and yelps. Finally, he got the white-haired man to calm down somewhat, and ascertained that the levity had its source in the latest session of the Council of Unity - to which Hieron had been conspicuously not invited.

"So what was it you decided in this secret meeting?" he demanded, not a little brusquely. He was privately quite put out that they had not seen fit to allow him to attend such an important meeting. Kiah fell silent, eyes glittering as he bit his lip childishly, savouring the moment of exposition.

"We made you Archon!" he exclaimed finally, eyes wide as he took in every detail of Hieron's impending reaction. The first stage of that reaction was confusion.

"Archon?" he echoed. "What the blazes is that?"

"Oh, just the supreme head of all Unity," Kiah informed him. "With power of veto over any Council decision, and the life and wellbeing of every Unity citizen in the palm of your hand." Hieron's reaction morphed into a mixture of shock and disbelief.

"Why in the name of the Creator would you do that?" he exclaimed. Kiah's expression changed from delight to hurt disapproval in an instant, the excitable child that had stood in his place succeeded by the familiar, serious adult.

"I will not tolerate blasphemy in my presence, my friend, no matter who you are. And I would appreciate it if you would take a moment to consider what an amazing gift this is that has been bestowed."

"A gift?" Hieron asked, agog. "I'd have thought that this was the kind of job that one would at least have to register some kind of interest in so as to be considered. What made you think I would want this much power and responsibility?" Kiah was visibly taken aback.

"Why on Earth would you not, dear boy?" he inquired, genuinely curious. "Besides, anyone applying to such a position would be the last person to be accepted in it; a yearning for absolute power is not a quality most people look for in their leaders, it seems."

"Well I can appreciate that," Hieron conceded. "But why me?"

"Because nobody else will do," Kiah answered. "Is it not obvious? You have been our spokesman ever since our first encounter with the array - since before the founding of Unity itself. People know you, and trust you - you were the one who told them about the alien threat when none of the corporations or the Earth government were willing to. And of course," he added with a slight smile, "you are the Hero of Tortuga."

Kiah left him with that thought, and it was one that went around and around in his head as he sat there alone in his quarters. How had he, of all people, made it to this point? Effectively in command of the vast majority of the human race? It was not something with which his mind would willingly cope. He had begrudgingly taken on the role of spokesperson because it had made sense at the time - Kiah had talked him into it, anyway. Why had Kiah now raised him to this exalted position? For all his talk of the Great Destiny, he had never seen the acolyte do anything that did not benefit him personally on some level. But if he had created this position to serve his ends, then why did he not simply place himself upon the throne? Perhaps it was another way of keeping his distance and avoiding accountability in the case that something went awry.

The thoughts were still tumbling through his mind when the door chime sounded again, and he greeted his former employer as he entered. Hieron resisted the urge to blurt out every thought that was spinning around in his head; he had no idea if he could still trust the tall, quiet man who had been in control of Arbiter Fuels for the past three decades. Perhaps the paranoia that was an inevitable side effect of his elevated position was already beginning to affect him. He waited for Parnett to speak first.

"Congratulations on your promotion," he began, the depth of his voice and flatness of his tone left ambiguous the matter of whether or not he meant his words seriously, mockingly, or ironically. "I always knew you were leadership material, and now I suppose I have the ultimate proof." He smiled slightly, his expression warm and friendly.

This helped Hieron to interpret his words more accurately, but the smile soon disappeared and Parnett's voice sank to hushed tones. "But I am here as a friend, to warn you to take this responsibility seriously. It is clear that the Sicarius' purpose in placing you in this position is to gain power for himself through manipulating you - and he is a master of that art. But I think he has underestimated your strength, and in doing so may have outplayed himself."

"You must seize the power that has been granted to you. Not just to put an end to the pathetic in-fighting that has divided the Council, but to make the galaxy a genuinely better place." He lowered his voice further, almost to a whisper. "I'm talking about the inequality between the core and the outlier worlds. Fat cats on Earth still enjoy veritable banquets day after day, while the miners on worlds like Galapagos - and even workers in my own refineries, Arbiter refining stations, go on the most meagre rations. Any questioning of their treatment is viewed as insurgency and dealt with accordingly. People - your people - are suffering and dying, and the Council doesn't even know."

"Then how do you know?" Hieron asked him, his tone as hushed as Parnett's. "And why don't you tell them?"

"I know because I listen," Parnett replied cryptically. "And I keep it to myself for two reasons: first, I very much doubt the Council would either believe me or do anything about it; second, I fear for my safety should I speak up. Which is another reason I needed to speak to you about your promotion - don't think you're beyond accountability now. While nobody can stop you doing whatever you like with Unity policy, if you publicly defy Sicarius' will, he may decide you are not well suited to the position any longer. It is no secret that the Predators are effectively in his direct employ."

The silence grew between them once Parnett had finished speaking, the tall man letting his words sink in. Finally Hieron looked him in the eye, fixing his green eyes upon Parnett's pale blues. "Did you know my wife well?" he asked quietly. Parnett shook his head, his expression showing faint traces of puzzlement.

"I met her, of course", he responded. "But we never really spoke of anything of any consequence."

"You would have liked her," Hieron smiled. "Her belief in equality and balance led her to constantly berate me about the oppression in the outlier systems. I always thought she was exaggerating things a bit."

"Believe me, Archon, she was not."

- - - - -

The first time Hieron truly enjoyed his new power was when he vetoed his own ascension ceremony. Kiah protested strenuously, insisting that the proceedings were absolutely necessary to establish his authority in the eyes of the populace. After an hour of his pestering and imploring protestations, Hieron finally agreed to have a minimal televised ceremony, but stood firm on the fanfares, robes, and draperies. Kiah accused him of having no sense of occasion, but reluctantly acquiesced.

The first few weeks were filled with such trivialities. There were attempts to move him to more opulent quarters, requests for photo opportunities, and suggestions of an official portrait. Soon, however, these fell into the background as the full reality of his new role was made apparent, with every decision and indecision of the Council run by him for approval, condemnation, or resolution. He half began to suspect that they were inventing work for him to either keep him busy or drive him mad; and both possibilities were at about equal odds.

The campaign against the pirates of the fringe systems continued, and it was not long before the Navy was back up to full strength - and indeed beyond - and able to effectively quell these minor annoyances without much difficulty. They continued to spring up, however, and Hieron demanded that the Council investigate what root causes there may be behind the defiance. He knew well enough, of course, but without the hard evidence he would not be able to get the Council behind him.

As time wore on, a pattern began to emerge. After each meeting of the Council, reduced now to once per week, he would expect a visit from Kiah, and one from Parnett. Normally these visits would be at least half a day apart, the tall CEO seeming concerned that the acolyte not discover his meetings with the Archon. Sicarius would invariably urge greater control over the Council, and a firmer stance in the outlier systems. He was also starting to argue in favour of formally establishing the Church as the state religion of Unity; while Hieron was aware that the vast and growing majority of his citizens were members of the Church, he was nevertheless reluctant to take that step.

Parnett's advice was usually a warning about Sicarius' agenda, and a plea for more to be done to equalise wealth in the galaxy and reduce the military presence in the fringe colonies. He claimed that resentment of the stringent rules and military enforcement was a major cause of the unrest plaguing those regions. Hieron assured him that he would like nothing more than to do as he asked, but his hands were tied by necessity: if he reduced the Navy numbers in a mining colony, they would have an armed rebellion on their hands within days. Parnett regarded him sadly when he heard those words, and warned him again that he should be resisting the influence of Sicarius and listening to his own feelings on the matter.

Hieron thought about what Parnett had said for days afterwards, and at the next Council session announced his intention to visit one of the fringe colonies personally. This was met with a great eruption of objections, most vocally from Kiah, who insisted that it would not be safe.

"I am quite capable of taking care of myself, Kiah," Hieron reassured him. "And it will be a lot safer if I go alone than with an ostentatious Navy escort." He waited until the fresh and even louder objections had died down, and stated simply, "I am the Archon, and this is my will. I want to see what's really going on out there, and the only way that will happen is by getting out there and using my own eyes. In fact," he added with a wide smile, "I'm leaving this very moment. Expect me back in two weeks. I'm sure I don't need to tell you where I'm going," he said quietly to Kiah as he passed him on the way to the door. "Your Predators will be able to tell you." He was not looking in the right direction to catch the acolyte's expression as he left, and perhaps if he had he would have thought again about his plan.

He ignored the salutes and stares as he crossed the main hangar of Alamo Station and climbed into his old Polecat. It had been so long since he had last flown it, but he knew it would come back to him as if he had stepped out of it only hours previously. Entering the destination into his navigational computer, he activated his EEG chip and went through the preflight sequence almost without thinking about it. When the Polecat leapt forward into the blackness of space, it felt like a rebirth. Despite the recycled nature of the air in the cockpit, he felt like he was able to breathe deeper and more satisfyingly than he had for months - or years. The freedom of space flight was one he had not even realised he had missed.

A few seconds was all it took him to reach safe jump distance from the station, as it was not in orbit of a planet and so had very little in the way of a gravity well. He felt the familiar lurch as his ship entered hyperspace, and he left the reality of meetings, arguments, and paperwork behind him. It would take more jumps than he had fuel for to get to his intended destination, as the Polecats were not designed for long-haul missions and only carried three jumps' worth. Thus, he planned to make a refuelling stop in the Scorpius system before the second part of the run to Thanatos; he could have simply travelled to Vulez, one jump away from Alamo Station, but that would not have been suitable. Its proximity to the base was one reason - it was probable there would be far less unrest in a system so close to the primary Navy base, after all; but also, it was likely that Kiah had guessed he would go there. He would not put it past the acolyte to have prepared a little play of what he wanted Hieron to see. He idly noted to himself that his paranoia was getting worse.

- - - - -

The refuelling in Scorpius passed without incident, Hieron joining the service queue waiting at the fly-by outlet on the underside of the orbital platform and taking on enough fuel for two more jumps. Most of the other ships in the system were merchants, and Hieron was glad to see that trade was still flourishing under Unity's governance. There were also a few Navy vessels in the vicinity, and while he made no move to overtly avoid them, he did make sure to keep an eye on the scanner to track their movements, ready for the smallest sign that they may have identified him. As far as he knew, the transponder aboard his Polecat was still set up to register as just another Navy fighter, and he hoped that none of the other pilots took it on themselves to query his assignment.

His luck held, though he secretly hoped it was because they had identified him and were allowing him to go about his business, rather than simply letting him slip through unchallenged. Security in these systems could not afford to be too lax, from what he had been told. Whatever the reason, he was not stopped as he made the jump to hyperspace, course set for his final destination. It took over an hour to make the jump, and as he waited in the cramped confines of the cockpit he could not help but think of the comm probes able to make the same jump in a tiny fraction of the time. If he knew Kiah, the acolyte was probably sending out messages to every agent he had in the galaxy informing them of Hieron's truancy.

Finally, he lurched out of hyperspace to find himself directly on course for docking at Thanatos V's primary refining station. There were several in orbit of the planet, of course - one station could hardly be expected to cope with the workload that the galaxy demanded - but one was larger than the others, to accommodate the amenities necessary to deal with everyday space traffic. There were also the living spaces for those who manned those amenities, and beds for any travellers that wished to make use of them. He began his approach, and signalled the docking authority of his intent to visit the station.

"Roger that, Polecat 176," came the response. "The pattern is free, and you are cleared to dock at docking port B. Welcome to Anubis Station."

Hieron began his final approach and lined himself up to fly through the opening doors of docking port B, attempting to mentally prepare himself for what was to come. It was quite inconceivable that he would be able to go completely unrecognised once inside the station, and he would have to have his wits about him; not for fear of assassination, as such - though that was a very real concern - but the diplomacy and endless formalities they would no doubt try to foist upon him as the Archon. Then he realised - he was the Archon, and with the entire force of Unity itself behind his every word, he could do just about anything he wanted. Including refusing to go through a lot of red tape and tedious ceremonies.

He was smiling as he made his way through the docking port's tunnels into the main hangar, passing through the scanners designed to detect certain forms of contraband such as drugs or personal weaponry. Finally he emerged into the main hangar and set his ship down in the space indicated on his navicomputer, releasing the canopy and climbing out into the mercifully open space of the hangar. The Polecat's cockpit truly was not designed to provide comfort over extended journeys, and he was starting to wish he had taken the time to stretch his legs while he was in Scorpius. A cheerful voice greeted him, and he braced himself as he turned to respond. It took a few seconds, but as Hieron finished returning the technician's greeting, the man's eyes widened, and it was clear that a connection

- and an interesting one at that - had been formed in his mind.

"Y-You're the Hero of Tortuga, aren't you sir?" he stammered, lowering his voice slightly as if not wanting to be overheard.

"That's what they call me," Hieron admitted with a sigh. "But you can call me Hieron - or Tomac, I answer to either."

"What are you doing here?" The man asked curiously, then thought about what he had just said to the leader of humanity, and how it might have come across. "Th-That is to say, what are - are you here becau - is it -" His face reddened as he went on, and Hieron put a hand on his shoulder in what he hoped was a reassuring manner.

"It's OK," he told the technician. "It was a fair question and politely asked. I am here to take a look at your facilities here on the station. An unofficial inspection, you might say."

The technician half nodded, half bowed, and pointed him in the direction of the administrator's office. He seemed only too glad to be out of Hieron's company, and Hieron could hardly blame him - with a shock like that it was remarkable he was even still able to form words. He hoped that the administrator had it a little more together, though, or this would be an awkward visit indeed. Finding the correct door, he knocked and was immediately summoned into the office beyond. The expression on the administrator's face was very similar to that which the technician had adopted upon recognising him in the hangar, except that it somehow looked more attractive and endearing on her. Hieron supposed he was biased.

"Welcome to Anubis Station, Archon," she said once she had managed to coax her vocal cords back into life. "Is there anything I can do to help you?" An administrator indeed, Hieron thought to himself; no accidental blurting of a possibly-offensive inquiry from this one. He smiled.

"Quite the contrary, Administrator," he assured her. "I was wondering if there was anything *I* could do for *you*." Her brow furrowed slightly in a frown and he guessed at her next words. "You see, I have been told that you might be having some problems out here with order and discipline, that sort of thing. Or rather, you would if you had fewer Navy enforcers in the region." It was important not to make her feel that he was concerned that she was finding the job difficult; her fear of losing her position of privilege would keep her from admitting that there were any problems at all. Of course, it was possible that his very presence would do that no matter what he said, but if he had simply arrived and started looking around on his own it might have caused great offence. The administrator looked rather confused still, but offered a reply.

"I am not sure what you have heard, Archon," she began defensively, "but our system is no more troubled than any at this distance from the core. There are always those who wish to live outside of the law, but that hardly makes us special does it?" Hieron groaned inwardly. This is what he had feared would happen.

"Not at all," he reassured her, taking a seat in the leather-lined chair across the desk from her own. "I am simply here to ascertain whether the current situation - or indeed the potential *future* situation - might warrant either an increase or a reduction in the current number of Unity troops allocated to your system. I don't want to hear your tourist-guide summary of the state of affairs, I don't even want your professional opinion on matters. I want your own honest, personal assessment of what's going on around here. What's your name?" She hesitated, taken by surprise.

"Um, Benerest" she answered. "Fara Benerest." He stood to lean over the desk and offered his hand, which she took uncertainly.

"Nice to meet you, Fara," he told her. "I'm Hieron." She nodded as he sat back in his seat. "That's what I want. I want Fara's opinion. What does Fara Benerest truly think about the situation here?"

"Well," she hesitated, "I suppose we've had a few problems here since Tortuga." She paused, clearly reminded by the word exactly who it was to whom she was talking. He nodded encouragingly for her to go on. "But most of that is because of the rationing. And pay," she added. "People are always complaining about their pay. I've not had many problems here that the Navy has had to help me with, though" she admitted. "But I don't know if that's just because people aren't unhappy enough to make the problems, or if it's the Navy's presence here that prevents them from doing anything." Hieron thought about that for a moment, eyes straying around the modestly decorated room as he did so. There were a couple of diplomas on the wall, as well as a shift chart and a large display screen; other than that, the walls were bare, and only a presumably personal picture in the electronic frame on her desk hinted that the Administrator thought of this space as her own.

"It is a bit ambiguous, isn't it?" he said eventually. "It could even be the case that the Navy's presence is what is causing the unrest that you do have. People don't like to feel that they're under somebody else's heel, and it's certainly not the image I would like to have associated with my... rule." He stroked his chin, feeling the first hints of stubble there. It had already been a long day. "Well, it sounds like any problems you have might be solved by raising wages or increasing rations for your people here. But as you say, who knows what is being suppressed purely by having the Navy here in your system?"

She looked at him uncertainly, not sure of where the conversation was going, nor if she would be able to object if she disagreed. He tried to reassure her with a friendly smile, but had the feeling that she could easily have interpreted that as an alligator's expression rather than that of a friend. "I came here to find out what was going on," he said finally. "I thought that the best way of achieving that would be to poke around quietly and try to gauge the mood directly from your people. But it's looking like I might be a little too well-known for that plan to work, and if you're right, I've already got what I came for."

He stood and shook her hand again in farewell, taking the few short steps to door before turning to face her once more. "A bit of friendly advice for you, Fara," he said. "If you're careful, you might be able to use this little visit to suggest that you are in close favour with the Unity administration. Of course, you might not want to associate yourself with us, and that's fine. Just letting you know that there could be some significant political capital to be had from people's knowledge of my visit here, and I won't object to you using it." He smiled again as she searched for a suitable response, and spared her the effort as he departed.

# Chapter 15

Kiah was furious. He expressed this by pacing like a man possessed, up and down the length of his quarters as he stung the air with expletives. He considered himself well-spoken, and his constant courtesy was a source of private personal pride, but he had not been this upset in as long as he could remember. What was Hieron thinking, going off on his own like that? As if he would be able to find out anything of use - his face was the most well-known in the entire galaxy, and Unity was feared even more than Hieron himself was admired. Everybody would tell him what he wanted to hear, and nothing more.

What was more galling than the trip itself, which presented very few problems practically speaking, was what it represented: he was losing him. Of course he knew about the surreptitious meetings with his former employer, Langton Parnett, but he had not considered the tall Arbiter CEO a true threat until now. If Kiah lost his hold on the new Archon, there was no telling what could happen - though with this latest talk of reducing troop numbers, he knew it would not go the way he wished. Furthermore, by referring to the Predators as a force exclusively under Kiah's control, Hieron had singled him out as a rival for his newly-granted power. Even if he had not intended to do so, the fact that he had said that in front of the whole of the Unity Council meant that they would see the two of them as rivals whether they were or not.

He had considered having his Predators stage a revolt of some kind aboard Anubis Station, but the risk that Hieron would see through it was too great; instead, he had instructed them to ensure his safety at all costs, because if there was one thing Kiah feared more than losing

Hieron politically, it was losing him physically. He did not often admit this fact to himself, but this was one of those rare times he allowed himself not only to swear, but to be honest with himself also. So it was with a tremendous confusion of emotions that he greeted Hieron as he walked into the acolyte's quarters; half of him wanted to strangle him out of frustration at his willfulness, and the other half wanted to embrace him as a brother, overwhelmingly relieved to see him alive. His emotions compromised, and he greeted him with a curt nod.

"So how was Thanatos?" he enquired. Hieron shrugged in response.

"More or less what I expected," he replied. "People aren't plotting revolution left, right, and centre, but they're not particularly happy either."

"Maybe they need more guidance," Kiah suggested carefully. "Another Minister or two -" Hieron held up his hand to stop him.

"Don't worry about suggestions, my friend," he told him. "I've already decided what I want to do. It's by way of an experiment in the Thanatos system. If it works, I'll look into the feasibility of making the change right across the board." He was smiling an open, friendly smile, and Kiah returned it. Finally, he had seen sense and was listening to reason.

"Yes, my friend!" he exclaimed with a grin. "I am glad to hear you say it. Once we make the Church the official established religion of Unity, we will finally bring in those fence-sitters who are sowing doubt in our people. It is fated to happen, but I welcome the ease with which you are submitting to the Great Destiny. It makes it so much easier when you let the Creator's plan move you like a leaf on the wind rather than standing like a rock in the current." He clasped Hieron's hand in his, and was for the final time hopeful that they could work together - that they could be partners.

The Hieron's expression hardened slightly, and Kiah's heart froze. "Not today, Kiah my friend. Perhaps one day we will do as you suggest, but my idea for Thanatos is to improve their lot. No more trade restrictions, no more rationing, a pay rise for everyone currently earning the minimum - you name it. Then we pull the Navy out of the system. Perhaps not entirely, but enough to remove the threat of overwhelming retaliation for any misconduct." Kiah snatched back his hand as if he had been stung.

"You'll destroy them!" he cried. "There will be anarchy! You think just because you've been there, and been treated to the utopian vision they want you to see, that you know how they will react to sudden and unexpected freedom?" He calmed himself with great effort, and began again in a more controlled tone. "Even if it works - which it won't - there is no guarantee that it would work for every settlement, and we truly do not have the resources for that much pay and food to suddenly hit the bills."

"Come now Kiah," Hieron chided him. "I think you know as well as I do that that's not even close to being true. Even if we don't cut back the military budget, which under these plans would be at least halved, we have more than enough wealth being channelled into the core systems to spare something for everyone. Equality, Kiah," he emphasised, taking the acolyte by the shoulders as if to shake sense into him. "True equality for the first time in galactic history." Kiah looked him in the eye.

"As I recall," he responded icily, "every historic attempt at economic equality on a large scale has not only failed but led to some impressive disasters. In every case, the system was abused, resulting in the suffering of millions and worldwide economic instability. I won't let you do the same thing to Unity!"

"Won't let?" Hieron retorted, his temper rising. "I thought I could do anything I wanted now I'm the almighty 'Archon' - or is it just anything that doesn't interfere with *your* plans? Am I a leader or a puppet?" he demanded.

"You're a leader, Hieron," Kiah replied softly, backing away and raising his hands in a conciliatory manner. "And leaders are supposed to listen to advice. The ones that heedlessly pursue their own goals are those that go down in the history books as tyrants. I know you well enough to know that that is not what you want - you want to be loved." A tenderness entered his expression and he took a step back toward Hieron.

"Perhaps," Hieron replied. "But what I really want is for any people under my rule, if I am to have one, to consider themselves free."

- - - - -

155

Eirik received his orders with no small amount of excitement; he had wondered if something like this would be happening ever since he had caught sight of the Archon visiting the station eight months previously. While he had the utmost respect for the man's military mind - he was the Hero of Tortuga after all - Eirik considered the man himself to be too weak for such a position of power. Such a man would never have the stomach to make the kind of decisions necessary to ensure peace and the success of Unity's goals. He was no politician, not like Sicarius. The white-haired acolyte had a subtle mind and an eye for opportunity, which were definitely traits that Eirik admired.

Anticipating the order, he had already begun preparations; he had expected it much earlier, in fact. When the Archon had appeared on the station he had assumed that the time had come for the plan to be put into action; but he trusted Sicarius' political instincts, and knew he had a much clearer idea of the big picture from his vantage point at Alamo Station. Eirik had had so long to prepare, in fact, that he was certain it could not fail; he had explored every contingency. The only danger had been the possibility that he could start to become attached to the subjects of his mission, but fortunately Eirik had never rated high on empathy tests. It had been one of the many factors that had elevated him to this position.

The mission had not been too difficult, of course; it was always easier to create unrest where there was already resentment and ill feeling. At last count he had manipulated almost half of the four hundred crew aboard the station into supporting the mounting mutiny, and the hardest part had been convincing the firebrands in charge to delay their action. They were angry and ready to move, but timing would be absolutely everything - on that much at least the brief had been unequivocal. A premature action could throw the entire plan off, and jeopardise the timely fulfilment Great Destiny itself.

It was time to visit with Adonye, he decided. The security chief had been the most impatient to make their move, and would welcome the news that the wait was very nearly over. Eirik walked, unhurried, through the station toward the security offices; it had been one of the earliest talents he had acquired, to walk as if nothing whatsoever was going on. It was harder than most people would think, but a completely vital skill for someone in his line of work. He returned a few salutes as he walked through the gleaming white corridors, recognising those that offered them as friend or foe as determined by his mental checklist.

Finally he reached the security offices, and as he entered Adonye dismissed the Lieutenant in attendance, whom Eirik noted would be on the other side when the time came. When he was sure she was a suitable distance away down the corridor, he closed the door and turned to the security chief.

"Tell me you've got a date for me," Adonye demanded. Eirik smiled. His was a bland face, which was another factor in his promotion; it became no more interesting or unique when he smiled.

"One week," he said, and the security chief returned his smile; hers though was bright and beautiful despite - or perhaps, Eirik thought, because of - the malicious glint in her eyes. There had been moments that Eirik had considered a liaison with her, but had decided that there was too much risk of compromise in that situation. It was the closest thing he had to a regret.

"Good," she smiled. "Everything's prepared, and everyone knows their role. This is going to be over before you can blink."

"Remember the directive," he admonished. "Casualties to a minimum."

"Oh, I remember," she responded, the smile fading to ice. "But I'd be far happier in carrying it out if I knew from whom this directive came. I know it's not you, so exactly who is it lending their support to this little insurrection?" Eirik looked her in the eye without responding for a moment, trying to gauge her disposition. It was an important aspect to the plan that as few of the 'enemy' be harmed, but resentment was high and it would be difficult to keep the firebrands in line. Perhaps it would be best to give her an answer, he decided.

"Very well," he said, reluctantly. "But only on the condition that it remains between us, and you impress the need for minimal casualties on the others." Adonye nodded in agreement. It hardly mattered if she kept it a secret or not, but telling her to keep it helped to reinforce the lie. "There is an alliance growing in the outlier systems, opposed to the rule of Unity - or specifically, the misrule of Unity. They are tired of the inequality between their systems and those at the core, and are ready to make their move against our oppressors. That is why the timing was crucial - not only is Unity planning to pull some of its forces from this system soon, but there are at least a dozen other systems planning their own 'little insurrections' to coincide with ours. If any one of them moves too early or too late, we give Unity the chance to strike back." Adonye had been taking this in with interest.

"So why minimal casualties?" she asked. "Surely we're going to have to fight the Navy eventually?"

"Perhaps," he responded. "But the initial plan is to take hostages and hold the station against their troops. If they have friendly personnel aboard the station, they are far less likely to attack the station with ships, so they will have to send soldiers, and we will have the advantage." Adonye smiled appreciatively, and Eirik idly wondered in a quiet corner of his mind if the plan, fake though it was, was turning her on.

- - - - -

Unaccustomed though he was to asserting his authority, Hieron was doing his best to learn quickly as he revealed his plans to the Council. He did not require their approval, but things would be made far easier if he could win it nonetheless. Kiah had made no secret of his opposition to the plan, but Hieron suspected that he would support him against the Council even so; they had developed a strange friendship over the years, and generally unpredictable though it was, Hieron felt that he could be sure of Kiah's reluctant vote in the Council.

Most of the others were vocal enough about their opposition to the plan, however. Parnett gave him a momentary and quiet look of approval as he finished outlining the idea, but it was like an oasis in a dry desert of incredulity and criticism. Silence fell as it came to Kiah's turn to speak, and Hieron groaned inwardly; it was demonstrative of their acceptance of the acolyte as the true power behind the Council, and indeed behind the position of Archon itself. Again he wondered why he had made Hieron Archon and not himself, as he surely could have done.

"It is a commendable plan," Kiah began, inclining his head respectfully to Hieron. "There are times that I think we do not consider the wellbeing of our citizens often enough in our deliberations and decisions, and it is both refreshing and humbling to be reminded of our solemn duty by the Archon himself." They all felt the 'however' approaching before he said it, and the majority of the Council smiled in satisfaction while Hieron's heart sank. Without Kiah's support, it would be very difficult indeed to carry out his plan. "However," Kiah inevitably continued, "to pull our forces out of a potential trouble spot is a highly dangerous action, not least for the personnel left behind. It is no secret that the higher levels of the command are resented for their somewhat higher salaries and access to more comfortable living conditions. What do you think would happen to them if we left them to the mob?"

"I don't think there is going to *be* a mob," Hieron argued. "Once we increase the wages and ship them some luxury foods and goods, they'll hardly be inclined to rebellion - and we're only withdrawing the Navy afterwards in any case. However high resentment may be, I doubt they are past the point of listening to reason; once they see our good intentions, it would be foolhardy in the extreme to jeopardise that."

"I believe you may be underestimating the depth of the resentment, Archon," Kiah told him in a low, steady voice that hinted of controlled anger. "These people have been -"

"Oppressed?" Hieron interrupted. "Is that what you were going to say? Because I seem to recall you assuring me that they were entirely 'sanguine' - your word I might add - about acquiescing to my rule. Are you telling me that you were misled? That perhaps your intelligence was faulty?" To his surprise, Kiah smiled at this.

"Quite the opposite, I assure you," he replied. "I was, at that time, merely trying to make the point that such action as you are currently planning would be both unnecessary and foolish."

"Well let me tell you, Sicarius," Hieron spat back, "I have visited Anubis Station *personally*, and what I saw there was a population that was neither sanguine nor kept barely in check. It was a group of people who believed they deserved more, and probably do. They will listen, and they will be better off." Kiah hung his head and sighed.

"I can see there is no deterring you on this, Archon," he conceded. "Very well, then let us plan this to the last detail, lest something untoward happen aboard Anubis."

# Chapter 16

A week later, the cargo vessel carrying the goods that were to be distributed to the personnel of Anubis Station arrived in the Thanatos system. The captain opened a comm link to the station and confirmed to the appropriate officer that they had arrived; this was acknowledged, so the captain closed the comm link and opened one to the message probe, sending back word to Alamo Station. He then proceeded to disable the entire communication system and bring the ship to a halt. Nobody would be talking to anybody else, and the ship would not be docking.

Aboard the Unity Navy's senior vessel in the system, similar events were unfolding. Noting that the cargo vessel had arrived and halted, the Admiral of the fleet sent word for all Navy vessels to withdraw to the Scorpius system. A dozen ships ceased patrols and made for safe jump distance, finally disappearing like lights winking out in the night.

On Anubis Station, Security Chief Adonye tapped her emergency access code into the comm system and disabled every other code on the network; she was now the only one who could authorise any exterior communications. She nodded to Eirik, and he pressed the button that would send a surreptitious signal out to the PDAs of every one of their people on the station. Within moments, the residential section was sealed off, the weapons lockers were secured, and the administrator was imprisoned in her office. Apologies were issued between friends, would-be heroes were relieved of their weapons, and not a single person was permanently harmed. Like clockwork, the uprising had simply ticked from one regime to another.

Eirik ensured that the message was dispatched to Unity stating they were no longer in control of the Thanatos system, and began the organising of the defences. It made most sense to concentrate their forces in the two main cargo bays; it was the only place that the Navy could land a significant number of troops, apart from the hangar - which was protected by multiple automated turrets, blast doors, and forcefields. Even if Unity managed to gain the hangar, they would have a hard time getting out into the rest of the station, and the defenders would have enough time to get into position ready for them.

Then it was a waiting game. It would take the Navy perhaps two hours to redeploy their Thanatos fleet with enough force to win back the station, and the main difficulty now would be keeping the defenders in line until then. Most had been frustrated by the no-kill order, and were itching to unleash the full force of their discontent upon their oppressors. A few of them spent the entire two hours feverishly pointing their weapons at the cargo bay doors.

Finally, Eirik's PDA flashed with a coded warning. The Navy was about to launch the assault. He made a show of checking the time, and told the defenders that the moment of truth should be upon them very soon. Adonye bellowed an order, and over a hundred weapons were raised, trained on the immense doors through which their enemy would inevitably pour. The security chief bellowed again, reminding them that their weapons would have little effect on the ships themselves, and to hold fire until the troops began to emerge.

Before long, an alarm sounded in the bay warning of someone attempting to override the door controls. Eirik, standing at the very rear of the cargo bay, slipped out quietly into the corridor as the huge doors opened like the gates of Hell. He had no wish to be in the cargo bay over the next few minutes, and made sure the door was sealed shut behind him. He felt nothing as the ship entered the cargo bay beyond, except a twinge of arousal as he imagined the beautiful Adonye gasping for breath in the noxious fumes now saturating the air. His mission was a resounding success, and would certainly ensure his progression within the Predators.

- - - - -

Kiah went personally to break the news to Hieron. Anubis Station had accepted the luxuries, it seemed, but as soon as the Navy withdrew there was an immediate and highly organised coup. It was only through poor tactical decisions on the part of the defenders, and a door malfunction, that the whole thing had been brought to a close and things returned to how they had been. The additional personnel were being shipped to the station immediately to replace those who had taken part in the uprising, and the few survivors from that group were being put to work in mines on the detention colonies. Hieron received all this information in silence, his expression giving away no hint of a reaction. He thanked Kiah and dismissed him.

It was too convenient, he mused to himself as he stood looking thoughtfully out at the stars from the porthole. Fully two metres across, it was symbolic of the opulence of his quarters; even the other Council members' quarters boasted windows of only half a metre at the most. He often spent long hours staring into the nothing outside, thinking deep thoughts as he watched the traffic come and go, the patrols swinging past as regularly as if they were attached to some immense carousel. His thoughts were rarely bright, though that was nothing new. Everyone he had counted as a true friend was dead, with the questionable exception of Kiah; he could not even remember the last time he had laughed. It was probably during the training for Tortuga, he reflected. Back when Vesta was still alive.

He wondered what had really happened in Thanatos. Making the relatively safe assumption that Kiah was lying to him about at least one aspect of the story, he saw two possible options: first, that the acolyte was covering up a massacre; second, that he was covering up a conspiracy. Considering the things of which he knew or suspected the white-haired man to be capable, it could easily be either one of those possibilities. The few things that Hieron was certain of were that his instructions had not been carried out, that this coup was artificially magnified if not outright manufactured, and that the circle of people whom he could safely trust was shrinking by the day.

He waited patiently, watching a Mastodon drift majestically past the station, the blue trident of Unity glowing ethereally on its flank. Eventually there was the inevitable chime at his door, and he called out for Parnett to join him, wondering if the CEO could be counted among his precious few friends or lost in the sea of those who wished him ill. Parnett entered and sat in one of the comfortable armchairs, looking inquiringly at Hieron until the Archon spoke.

"He claims it was a coup," Hieron told him. "A very organised one that struck the minute the Navy withdrew. A majority of the station crew were involved, apparently, but the Navy got back and quashed it fairly peacefully."

"Do you believe that is what happened?" Parnett asked him quietly.

"How am I supposed to know what to believe?" Hieron retorted with a bitter laugh. "That's why I went to Thanatos in the first place - to see with my own eyes. At this rate I'm going to need another thousand pairs of eyes to witness for myself what's going on in this galaxy. And I don't mean spies - I mean my own physical eyes with a direct link to my brain. I can't trust anyone any more, it seems."

"You just have to be careful about choosing your friends," Parnett reassured him. "Sicarius is a poor choice," he added.

"But I can trust you?" Hieron asked, sitting opposite Parnett. "How am I supposed to make that kind of decision?"

"All you can do is consider what facts you do have, and try to trust your instinct," the taller man said. "To your knowledge, have I ever acted against your best interests?" Hieron looked him in the eye for a long while before replying, his look met steadily by the CEO's grey gaze.

"No," he answered finally. "As far as I know, you have always acted in the best interests of the corporation, and of the galaxy. With the possible exception of voting for me to be made Archon, I can think of no example in which your actions have harmed me in any way. But that's just it," he said, leaning forward and lowering his voice as if wary of being overheard. "It's the things I don't know about that could hurt me. I don't know for certain of any time Kiah has acted against me."

"And yet here you are, lowering your voice in case he hears you, speaking of distrusting his account of what happened aboard Anubis Station. Furthermore, you are confiding in me, whom you claim you have no more or less reason to trust than Sicarius. Those are your instincts, Hieron. You need to listen to them more closely." He stood, and Hieron followed him to the door. "Sicarius will do anything to increase his power, and that of his precious Church. At the moment, that involves increasing the power of Unity itself - hence the Anubis coup. But before long he will move to make the Church a more central aspect of the government, and you will have to decide whether you want to help him or hinder him. There will be no middle way for the Archon."

The door slid shut behind him, and Hieron was left alone with his thoughts again.  On the whole, he decided, he preferred to have company.

- - - - -

As the Council was called to order, Hieron could not keep Parnett's words out of his head and saw the truth of them in everything Kiah said.  The majority of the agenda was taken up with discussing the failed coup in Thanatos, and the implications for the galaxy as a whole.  Naturally, Kiah pointed out, it could hardly have gone better for Unity - they had demonstrated not only their generosity but also the futility of defiance.  Though it was a shame, he admitted, that their magnanimity had been met with such ingratitude, it was a vain hope that it would have gone otherwise.  He did not say that he had opposed the plan on these very grounds to begin with, but the implication was there for all to hear.

"Nevertheless," he continued, "the message that we must take from the events aboard Anubis Station is clear - certain citizens are still, despite all our efforts, able and willing to openly defy the will of the majority.  From the extensive research I have had carried out on behalf of this Council, I have found that those places with the greatest unrest are those with the lowest rates of Church attendance overall." This elicited groans from a few mouths around the table.

"We have been over this a great many times, Sicarius" Parnett stepped in.  "Without visiting the reliability of your sources, there is no reason to suppose that just increasing the number of preachers in these colonies will have a significant effect on their faith, let alone the tenuous link that faith might have with obedience.  So unless you have a new tune to sing us -"

"I do, as a matter of fact" Kiah snapped, the acidity of his tone dissolving what little idle murmuring chatter there had been in the background.  Hieron watched with interest as Parnett impassively returned the acolyte's vengeful glare.  "I want to establish Intentional Creation as the official state religion of Unity," he declared to the Council at large.  Hieron was somewhat taken aback by this announcement; though he had often raised the possibility in their private meetings, Kiah had always  mentioned it in the tones one uses for an afterthought, or a curious hypothetical. This was the first time he had ever voiced the idea in the presence of others, as far as Hieron knew, and he had done so knowing his general opposition to it.

Parnett gave Hieron a significant look before replying, its meaning all too clear. "With all due respect, I hardly feel that is appropriate. Your own research shows that the majority of those not attending Church services are doing so because they belong to one of the Fringe Faiths, or are self-declared non-fatalists. Establishing Intentional Creation will serve only to alienate them further, and deepen the problems."

"Quite the contrary, Mr Parnett," Kiah assured him, smiling his chillingly humourless smile. "Once we have established faith as a cornerstone of what it means to belong to a unified, harmonious, and happy society, it will become undesirable in and of itself to set oneself apart. People *want* to belong, and so all we have to do is make faith an inseparable part of belonging."

"What of freedom, Kiah?" Hieron was surprised to find that the words had made their way quietly out of his own mouth. "What of a citizen's right to choose their own faith, or to choose that they have none?" Kiah glanced at him, clearly as surprised as Hieron at his uncharacteristic rebuke.

"They will of course remain free to choose whichever path they so wish," the acolyte replied. "We are simply making it easier and more acceptable for them to choose the correct path."

"I don't think that freedom to choose the government line is a freedom worth having," Hieron responded. "And until you give me a coherent argument of why it is in the best interests of the citizens of this galaxy to have one established state religion, I will not condone its establishment." His heart rate had doubled while he spoke, as he realised that he was drawing a line in the sand against an undoubtedly dangerous opponent. Kiah's eyes were wide with surprise and anger as the same realisation hit him.

"It seems you have made your decision, Archon," he spat, the malevolence in his voice barely masked. "I will of course do my best to persuade you that this is indeed the course of wisdom. If, however, you are determined to persist in this folly, I suppose I will have to revisit my plans." With that, he strode out abruptly, white curls bouncing as he went. The Council exchanged significant glances. While most had simply faded into the background during the last few years, leaving the discussions in the hands of those with the real power, not one of them had failed to keep their ear to the ground. All of them grasped the magnitude of what had just happened, and individually resolved to make quiet preparations for whatever was to follow.

- - - - -

It was Hieron himself who found Langton Parnett hanging by a thin cord from one of the heavy light fittings in his quarters. His face was purple, and although the smell was nearly overpowering, it was not the stench of death and decay - only the usual malodour of a body losing control of its muscles. It was two days since the last Council meeting, the one in which Hieron had openly defied Kiah alongside Parnett, and trying to see his mentor's apparent suicide as a coincidence was stretching the bounds of probability to well-nigh breaking point. There was only a small corner of his mind that still doubted whether Kiah had been responsible for Parnett's death.

He ordered the body cut down and made ready for a state funeral. It was an empty gesture, but it was all he had left to offer the former CEO. As they removed Parnett's corpse in a long, opaque pod, Hieron crossed the room to the desk, activating the PDA there on the off-chance there had been a suicide note or a message that would explain what had happened. The screen remained blank. It seemed that Parnett had seen fit to destroy all of his personal data prior to his death, leaving nothing but a blinking cursor behind.

But then the cursor started to move. Crossing the screen from left to right, it left behind a trail of letters that made the Archon's heart race.

> So I am dead. I wondered if it would come to this. I hope it is you reading this, Hieron. You must continue our work. You must thwart his plans. If you can't do that, then for Christ's sake avenge me!

There was no doubt, then. Kiah had murdered Parnett, or more likely had him murdered by one of his assassins, all because he had been counselling Hieron against him. It was both terrifying and not a little intoxicating to think that he was so important. The waves of grief over his friend and mentor's death crashed ineffectually against the walls he had built up; he was used to losing friends. One more would hardly make a difference.

Making his way to his quarters, he thought over Parnett's final message that the CEO had somehow programmed into his PDA. He was now more determined than ever to continue to oppose Kiah openly in the Council; if the acolyte had thought that Parnett was the true power behind Hieron's newfound adamance, then he had risked showing his hand for nothing. However, Hieron had to anticipate his next move, or the game could be over before he knew it.

As far as Kiah knew, he reasoned, Hieron would now be awash with grief and lacking guidance - his next move would certainly be to offer his support in a diplomatic manner. He would no doubt apologise for the outbursts at the last session of the Council and suggest a truce of some kind while Hieron absorbed this latest blow. He decided that his best defence may well be to play along for the time being, allowing Kiah to believe that Parnett's death had hit him as hard as the massacre following the first encounter with the array had done.

But then, he thought, perhaps it would be better to take him entirely by surprise by confronting him; it was the last thing the acolyte would be expecting, and could work by that virtue alone. Kiah did not cope well with surprises.

Which left only the question of what to do with the advantage once he had gained it. Blackmail Kiah using his knowledge of the murder? That was an unlikely tactic to say the least - Hieron was not certain, but thought it was possible that the Archon was only the second most powerful figure in the government. Murder accusations would be a simple thing for Kiah to avoid or deflect. He had to find some way of fulfilling Parnett's final wish - of that much at least he was certain. But aside from continued defiance, he had no idea how else to accomplish those ends. Kiah Sicarius still held all the cards.

Then there was the matter of avenging his former mentor. The message had made it clear enough that it was intended as a contingency plan only - for the event that he failed to achieve their aims through any other means. But the more he thought about it, the more he wondered if there were any other means by which he could thwart the supernaturally determined acolyte. If he were willing to kill to achieve his ends, then perhaps it was only by the same methods that he might be stopped.

# Chapter 17

Kiah took a deep breath before pressing the chime for the door to Hieron's quarters. He had been here countless times before, but never had the impending conversation been so vitally important. One word wrong, one slip of his tone even, and his facade could be blown. There were too many reasons why that must not happen, and even his continued dominance of Unity did not rate highest on the scale of importance. If he played his cards right, he could have everything he had ever wanted by the time he came back out through these doors.

It boded ill for his control of the situation when Hieron answered the door immediately and in person, rather than the delayed response from the bed that Kiah had expected. Had Parnett meant so little to him? Perhaps he had made a miscalculation somewhere along the line, and Parnett had been less of an influence on the Archon than he had suspected. But no, the surveillance tapes were quite clear in showing the extent to which the former CEO of Arbiter Fuels was responsible for the defiant direction of Hieron's recent activity. He forced a sympathetic smile in greeting and delivered his planned opening line.

"Hieron. How are you holding up?" The Archon waved him inside and seemed to genuinely consider the question before replying in a strong, steady voice.

"I'm doing well, all things considered," he told Kiah, indicating for the acolyte to sit. Kiah politely refused. "I mean, I discovered the corpse of a friend this morning, but other than that my day's going really rather well." The acolyte did not fail to detect the tone in Hieron's voice, but thought it best to play along with the obvious charade for the time being. Whatever he was concealing with his seemingly lighthearted manner could be any of several things, and possibly quite benign.

"It couldn't have been easy for you, my friend," he sympathised carefully. "I know how much the old man meant to you."

"Yes, it was a bit of a shock" Hieron conceded, and paused, fixing Kiah with a level stare as if he were trying to determine guilt or innocence. "You know what I found most shocking, though?" he continued finally. Kiah shook his head, which was followed by another, only slightly shorter, pause. "That you didn't make it look like a heart attack."

The atmosphere in the spacious quarters changed irrevocably. Tension between the two of them, bubbling quietly under the surface throughout their conversation, was suddenly filling the air and making it harder to concentrate. Kiah groped for the appropriate response, considering and rejecting various forms of denying the implied accusation. Honesty could be the only tactic, but it had to be carefully presented. He had planned to tell Hieron everything anyway, so this was his chance. He was being given the opportunity to explain his actions.

"I had hoped it would suggest that your joint course of action was doomed," he explained finally, watching closely Hieron's reaction for any hint of how his words were being received. The Archon simply stared impassively back at him, giving nothing away. The acolyte suddenly felt very small in his presence, but found it a not-uncomfortable sensation. "Everything I have done, I have done for you, Hieron," he continued. "I killed Parnett because he was driving a wedge between us, and leading you down a path that would only end in your own demise." Still no reaction showed on the Archon's face, but Kiah thought he saw his fists clench ever so slightly. Not a promising sign, and time for a new tactic.

"I have done so much for you," he railed. "I made you ruler of the galaxy! I expected only a little comradeship in response, and instead you question my wisdom in matters with which you have been acquainted for but a fraction of your life. Ever since I was plucked from the crib and chosen as the Primus' assistant, I have known only politics. Power is in my blood and I can smell my way through a situation you would have to spend a day to work out, and yet you question my wisdom on the best way to run this government? A government that would not exist were it not for me? How can you not see that at every turn, at every crossroads, I thought of you? I could have left you in obscurity, scraping a living and an identity from the squabbling mess that was the corporate militias. But instead I raised you up, higher than you had a right to expect, and now you betray me?"

His impassioned speech left him emotionally drained, and he stood breathing heavily. But still Hieron's face showed no reaction to his words. Kiah wondered if the end truly had come; would he be forced to eliminate this final hurdle to power? Would this be the final Test the Great Destiny had in store for him? He was not certain he was up to the task. Then Hieron spoke, snapping him out of his reverie.

"Why me?" The words hung in the tense air between them, simple and profound, the doorway to the truth that Kiah had fought so hard to conceal. The one person who had guessed at the answer to that question was now long dead. Honesty here could destroy one or both of them, or it could set them free. The two men stared at each other as the question hanging over them grew impatient for a response.

- - - - -

Kiah looked for all the world like a small animal caught in a trap, his thin frame slightly bent forward still from his prior outburst, his white hair dishevelled and dark eyes wide. Clearly Hieron's question had taken him somewhat off-guard, as he had calculated it might. He had been so defensive that a potentially generous offer to explain himself had been unexpected. Even so, Hieron thought, his hesitation was starting to surpass mere surprise and instead hint at some deep and personal truth that his question might reveal. This was unexpected to say the least: he thought he knew the one and sole reason that Kiah did everything, namely the acquisition of power for himself. He had all but admitted that much already. The more he thought about it, however, the more he came to realise that there were indeed actions of Kiah's that could not be simply and easily explained by lust for power alone. For the first time since their confrontation had begun, Hieron started to wonder if he might actually learn something about the acolyte.

"You had great talent," Kiah's quiet voice answered finally, almost

171

making Hieron jolt with surprise. The silence had grown strong and he had nearly become lost in his own thoughts.

"Your talent for speaking to people was something I could never hope to replicate," the acolyte continued. "Without you, the cause would have fallen on deaf ears and we would have been lost. You believed in cooperation from the start, and you were able to convince others to do the same."

Hieron considered this and how plausible it seemed, turning it this way and then that in the privacy of his own mind, while he kept his face intentionally expressionless. False modesty aside, Hieron could accept that his talent for explaining and persuading was probably somewhat greater than most, certainly; but could this alone account for his being singled out by Sicarius as the focus of his considerable attentions? There was surely more to it than a simple talent for persuasion. "You had easy enough access to the CEOs," he countered. "All of whom - with the possible exception of Ari Zack - had more than enough experience of corporate politics, and therefore possessed significant skills at manipulating others, whether through persuasion or less direct means. Why not choose one of them as your Archon?" Kiah seemed to have been expecting this question, as he responded immediately, almost eagerly.

"And they also had years of experience using those skills for political ends. I needed someone with raw talent to take under my care and raise personally through the political hierarchy. If I had singled out any one of the CEOs, they would have either turned on me or it would have encouraged too much resentment among the rest of the Council." His manner was becoming more confident as he explained this, and Hieron could not help but feel that he was losing the advantage in this opaque conversational duel.

The acolyte had seized too keenly upon this strand of discussion regarding Hieron's talent; perhaps that suggested that the core of truth Hieron sought lay in another direction entirely. Of course, it was also possible that he was simply relieved that he was being given the chance to explain rather than being confronted outright. He would have to probe a little deeper. But without a solid example of something Kiah had done that did not square with his excuses, that would not be easy. He decided to bluff.

"Kiah, my friend," he said softly, even gently, as he took a step toward him as if in a gesture of comfort. "I think we both know there's more to it than that." As if his words were those of a spell, a sudden change came over the acolyte standing opposite him. He watched their magic twist his expression through several distinct emotions, some of which he would find it hard to put a name to, before they finally settled into something between relief and a quiet, tentative euphoria.

- - - - -

In the ceiling, the only witness to the proceedings gazed lifelessly from a plastic lens, concealed in the light fixture next to the window. It took in the two figures, engaged as they seemed to be in some kind of complex dance, each taking steps forward or steps back, arms waving in turn. Then the one that was often here said something and the action stopped. The frozen figures faced each other in a silence which grew between them until finally the white-haired man spoke, quiet words drifting up into the microphone accompanying the lens.

"Y-You know?" he stuttered, receiving a simple nod in response. "For how long?"

"I worked it out only recently," Hieron replied after a slight hesitation.

"Before or after, uh..." Kiah seemed to be searching for the right words. "...the last Council session?"

"What?" Hieron asked, his hesitation clearer this time. "Oh, definitely after." At those words, all the tension seemed to drain out of the acolyte, and he sagged visibly with relief.

"Oh, thank God," he gasped. "I thought keeping it bottled up inside would kill me." The white-haired acolyte flopped down to sit on the edge of the bed. "You know, there are times even I doubt the Great Destiny," he confided. "I consulted the threads of fate relentlessly, every time I meditated, on how this very conversation might end. Every time it gave a different answer, as if this were the one thing in the universe that the Great Destiny had no plan for in its great tapestry. But now I know it was simply shielding it from me because had I known the outcome, it would have dampened the joy of the moment." A tired but euphoric smile played about his mouth as he spoke. Hieron, meanwhile, had hardly moved except to adopt a slight, hesitant smile in return.

173

"Still, you don't need to hear my problems," Kiah continued, and patted the bed next to him. "Come here and let's talk for a while." His expression was hopeful but fragile, as if the slightest hint of rejection would destroy him. Hieron took a step toward the bed, his expression slowly showing realisation dawning. As the acolyte stood and took Hieron's hands in his own, that realisation became complete and he stood staring at the other man as if expecting to wake up at any moment. Kiah meanwhile seemed not to notice this reaction at all in his rapture. Finally, Hieron broke the spell with a soft but barbed voice.

"Is this why you killed my wife?" Like venomous spikes, the words punctured the moment and left it paralysed. Then, slowly, the poison worked its way between the two men and Kiah's expression took on a sickly cast as he stumbled back a step, his hands slipping from Hieron's. The Archon himself, meanwhile, was also digesting this realisation and appeared to have taken the acolyte's reaction as an admission of guilt. Tears welled in his eyes, and his expression went from horrified to sickened. "You murdered my wife and child, sent them to their deaths - just so you could pursue me without competition?" His voice grew steadily stronger and more aggressive as he spoke. Grief was turning to anger.

"She was turning you against me," Kiah protested, his voice small and weak, his body shrinking back under Hieron's accusatory gaze.

"So you had her eliminated, like you did with Parnett, and your predecessor. I suppose I should think myself lucky that I was the object of your ambition rather than an obstacle to it. I doubt I'd have survived this long otherwise."

"Please understand," Kiah begged, a modicum of strength returning to his voice in defiance of the Archon's verbal onslaught. "I did everything with your - and my - best interests at the forefront of my mind. When you went off on that fool's errand to Anubis Station, I barely slept out of worry for what might happen - I knew how dangerous it was, after all. I have never wished you any harm, and any sadness I may have caused you was only in the course of doing what I thought was best. I know the idea might take some getting used to, and I don't blame you for being angry - I know now that concealing my feelings was the worst thing I could have done - but I would very much like you to just think about things for a while."

"Think about things?" Hieron demanded, steel in his voice and tears rolling down his cheeks. "You murdered my wife and child to have me for yourself, and you want me to actually consider acquiescing to this? You want me to tell you that all is forgiven, that I agree with everything you've done? I've got a better idea." He picked up his steak knife from the table where it had been sat waiting for dinner, and gripped it tight in his right hand. "How about you set about paying me for what you've taken?"

Fear lit up Kiah's eyes and set his body in motion, lunging at the bigger man before he had a chance to strike. The knife scored up his left arm as he attempted to wrest it from his attacker's grip, and Hieron's forehead came smashing down on the acolyte's nose, breaking the skin and starting a slow crimson flow down his face. Kiah reeled and barely regained his balance in time to fend off another assault, sinking his fist into Hieron's stomach and winding him. The knife dropped to the floor and both men made a grab for it, Hieron successfully kicking it away toward the bed and bringing his knee up in one movement to connect with Kiah's chin.

The acolyte sprawled on the floor and Hieron bent to pick up the knife again. Kiah, however, was faster getting back on his feet than he had expected, and before Hieron could turn back to face him, one of the dining chairs connected sharply with the back of his head. He dropped to the floor, dazed and gasping, the knife knocked again from his hand.

"I understand your anger, Hieron," Kiah panted, dabbing a sleeve at his face and blinking against the dizziness. "I have made too many mistakes over the past ten years, but I don't want us to throw it all away in the heat of the moment like this. Cool off and then come to see me. We'll talk this out properly." He started toward the door, but stopped as he heard a bitter, mirthless laugh.

"You think I'm going to change my mind?" Hieron spat, levering himself with difficulty to his feet. "Even if your hands were clean of the blood of my friends, I would not want you. You use people, you see nothing but your own ambition - even when you look at someone you think you could love. Your blind adherence to that superstitious nonsense you call a religion is just a convenient excuse for your megalomaniacal warmongering. You're a truly despicable human being, and humanity would be well rid of you."

Kiah stood in the frame of the closed door, his back to the man he loved, his tears drying and muscles tensing. "So be it," he said, with sad resolution. By the time Hieron realised his mistake, the knife was already in the acolyte's hand and he was advancing toward him purposefully. The Archon managed to deflect the first few thrusts, once sending his fist flying blindly into the side of Kiah's head. As he did so, however, the knife came around under his swing and sunk deep between the ribs on his right side. Kiah's face remained impassive as the blood sprayed forth from his former friend's lips, and he ignored the hands that grasped desperately at his throat as he drove the knife into Hieron's chest again and again.

# Epilogue

There was no funeral. Traitors, the new Archon claimed, deserved no such honour. None failed to note the lesson being given in his single-handed personal execution of the most powerful man in the galaxy. A few short months later, the Council of Unity was completely dismissed and re-formed, with specific ministries in charge of the different aspects of running the government. The transition was a quiet one, as quiet as the orders that doubled the production of ships for the Navy and the training of soldiers.

Klaira received the news with, at best, mixed feelings. Hieron had betrayed her when she was at her most vulnerable, after all, but he had still been her husband, and a good man beside that. She had faith that Kiah would do his best for the galaxy, but she could not forget that it was he who had been recommending the measures that would severely curtail the freedom of people under Unity's rule.

The shuttle stood waiting on the landing pad, rain sweeping in waves across the scene as she stepped out into the storm. The little hand she held gripped her tighter, though whether it was due to fear of the severe weather or excitement at the thought of boarding the shuttle, she was unsure. Together they ran across the tarmac to the shelter of the shuttle's port wing, which shaded the airlock. The captain was waiting for them, and greeted their arrival with a salute and a warm smile. He assured them that their belongings had already been loaded into the cargo hold, and they were ready to leave just as soon as she liked.

She nodded gratefully in response, still not entirely used to the level of service that her current wealth could afford her. A parting gift from

Kiah, the credits had been more than useful over the years, and she had invested them wisely; this was why she could afford a privately-chartered shuttle to take them to their new home. It was not that Centauri was an unsuitable home, or that they had not been made welcome in Thessa, the primary colony. Indeed, there had been many tearful goodbyes and promises to stay in touch when she had broken the news to her close circle of friends. But Thessa was a large settlement by colonial standards, and she wanted her child to grow up somewhere with clear air and trees.

They stood at the main viewport on the observation deck as the whine of the engines grew, the technician in her noting with satisfaction that every minutest sound was as it should be. Then they were airborne, and a pair of tiny hands pressed themselves against the glass as a pair of tiny eyes watched the ground recede beneath them. In virtually any other ship, they would have to be strapped in against the G-forces as they reached escape velocity; this top-of-the-range shuttle, however, was fitted with the latest in inertial dampeners and they hardly felt a thing as they accelerated out of the atmosphere. Idly she wondered if the captain would let her take a look at the new systems while they were en route.

Sinking down into the indecently comfortable chair, she took a moment to remember the man she had loved, and suppressed the usual feelings of anger out of respect for the dead. Had he deserved the end he had met? Probably not, she decided, at least not for anything he had done to her alone. And as far as politics were concerned, his heart had always seemed to be in the right place, though he did allow himself to be led too easily.

His child would have questions soon, she knew, though she had not yet decided what to tell him.

# Acknowledgments

As this is the first novel published in set in the universe of the Unity Chronicles, it is here that I must note a major source of inspiration for the series as a whole: Ambrosia Software's superlative 1996 game *Escape Velocity*. It inspired me, at the age of perhaps thirteen, to pen the first thirty pages of what turned out to be the seeds of The Unity Chronicles. They're still churning out great software - leisure and otherwise - so do check out their website at www.ambrosiasw.com.

As for this particular tome, the majority was written under great pressure during the National Novel Writing Month (or NaNoWriMo) 2009, which leads me to acknowledge the event itself for finally providing the motivation to knuckle down and bash out an actual novel instead of obsessing over the background for the universe itself. It also necessitates thanking everyone who might have suffered from neglect as tapping away on my laptop consumed my every waking moment. You know who you are.

Finally, to all those who offered feedback on ideas, or provided tolerant smiles and nods in the face of relentless blathering on my part, my thanks also.

Oh, and thanks for buying it!

www.ingramcontent.com/pod-product-compliance
Lightning Source LLC
Chambersburg PA
CBHW060108260626
47160CB00005B/1827